BARRON'S BOOK NOTES

GUSTAVE
FLAUBERT'S

Madame Bovary

BY

Lewis Warsh

SERIES COORDINATOR

Murray Bromberg
Principal, Wang High School of Queens
Holliswood, New York

Past President
High School Principals Association of New York City

BARRON'S EDUCATIONAL SERIES, INC.
Woodbury, New York • London • Toronto • Sydney

ACKNOWLEDGMENTS

Our thanks to Milton Katz and Julius Liebb for their contribution to the *Book Notes* series.

All inquiries should be addressed to:
Barron's Educational Series, Inc.
113 Crossways Park Drive
Woodbury, New York 11797

Library of Congress Catalog Card No. 85-4075

International Standard Book No. 0-8120-3524-0

Library of Congress Cataloging in Publication Data
Warsh, Lewis.
  Gustave Flaubert's Madame Bovary.

  (Barron's book notes)
  Bibliography: p. 118
  Summary: A guide to reading "Madame Bovary" with a
critical and appreciative mind encouraging analysis of
plot, style, form, and structure. Also includes
background on the author's life and times, sample tests,
term paper suggestions, and a reading list.
  1. Flaubert, Gustave, 1821–1880.   Madame Bovary.
[1. Flaubert, Gustave, 1821–1880.   Madame Bovary.
2. French literature—History and criticism]   I. Title.
II. Series.
PQ2246.M3W3   1985   843'.8   85-4075
ISBN 0-8120-3524-0

567   550   987654321

CONTENTS

HOW TO USE THIS BOOK

You have to know how to approach literature in order to get the most out of it. This *Barron's Book Notes* volume follows a plan based on methods used by some of the best students to read a work of literature.

Begin with the guide's section on the author's life and times. As you read, try to form a clear picture of the author's personality, circumstances, and motives for writing the work. This background usually will make it easier for you to hear the author's tone of voice, and follow where the author is heading.

Then go over the rest of the introductory material—such sections as those on the plot, characters, setting, themes, and style of the work. Underline, or write down in your notebook, particular things to watch for, such as contrasts between characters and repeated literary devices. At this point, you may want to develop a system of symbols to use in marking your text as you read. (Of course, you should only mark up a book you own, not one that belongs to another person or a school.) Perhaps you will want to use a different letter for each character's name, a different number for each major theme of the book, a different color for each important symbol or literary device. Be prepared to mark up the pages of your book as you read. Put your marks in the margins so you can find them again easily.

Now comes the moment you've been waiting for—the time to start reading the work of literature. You may want to put aside your *Barron's Book Notes* volume until you've read the work all the way through. Or you may want to alternate, reading the *Book Notes* analysis of each section as soon as you have finished reading the corresponding part of the original. Before you move on, reread crucial passages you don't fully understand. (Don't take this guide's analysis for granted—make up your own mind as to what the work means.)

Once you've finished the whole work of literature, you may want to review it right away, so you can firm up your ideas about what it means. You may want to leaf through the book concentrating on passages you marked in reference to one character or one theme. This is also a good time to reread the *Book Notes* introductory material, which pulls together insights on specific topics.

When it comes time to prepare for a test or to write a paper, you'll already have formed ideas about the work. You'll be able to go back through it, refreshing your memory as to the author's exact words and perspective, so that you can support your opinions with evidence drawn straight from the work. Patterns will emerge, and ideas will fall into place; your essay question or term paper will almost write itself. Give yourself a dry run with one of the sample tests in the guide. These tests present both multiple-choice and essay questions. An accompanying section gives answers to the multiple-choice questions as well as suggestions for writing the essays. If you have to select a term paper topic, you may choose one from the list of suggestions in this book. This guide also provides you with a reading list, to help you when you start research for a term paper, and a selection of provocative comments by critics, to spark your thinking before you write.

THE AUTHOR AND HIS TIMES

Already disappointed with humanity by the age of twenty-two, Gustave Flaubert abandoned the outside world and retired as a hermit to his family's estate in the small town of Croisset, France. It was in this provincial Normandy setting that he created one of the world's great novels, *Madame Bovary*, and in which he spent most of his life almost mystically devoted to literature. Since he was deeply affected by stress and believed that a life of activity would damage the creative process, he wanted to shut the door, close off all distractions, and bury himself in work.

Yet Flaubert was not an altogether unsocial man. He kept an apartment in Paris for the winter months, entertained friends, traveled periodically, and enjoyed being a favorite of Princess Mathilde, cousin of the Emperor of France. He never wrote for fame or money, but nonetheless enjoyed the glory his success brought—and if you see this as a contradiction to his need for seclusion, then you've already spotted one of several major conflicts within this talented writer.

Born on December 12, 1821, Flaubert was the son of a prominent surgeon in Rouen, France. Having spent much of his childhood in the grim environment of the hospital where his father worked, he had an idea of the gruesome pain and suffering that plagued the sick. He also had a good idea of the incompetence that plagued the medical profession. This early exposure to human frailty and professional mishaps no doubt contributed to Flaubert's general pessimism about life, but it also provided the solid background of medical and scientific information he drew upon to describe the middle-class medical practitioners in *Madame Bovary*. The bungled clubfoot operation on the stable boy, for example, resembles incidences of malpractice he had encountered in real life.

Another result of Flaubert's familiarity with medicine (his brother Achille was also a doctor) was his awareness that middle-class lip service to science and progress could be mere pretentious nonsense. While he believed in true science, he was wary of people, like the pharmacist Homais, who invoked the spirit of progress to justify their own comfortable positions in society.

Flaubert's youth coincided not only with the rise of the bourgeoisie during the reign of King Louis-Philippe (1830–48), but with the period of Romanticism. This literary and artistic movement, begun in the late eighteenth century, rejected the predominant view of that century's thinkers that "reason" was the guiding principle of life and man's most important attribute. French education was still grounded in the previous century's ideals, so that its models of art and literature were from the classical world of ancient Greece and Rome—a world that glorified the rational. The Romantics reacted by "rediscovering" other sides of life. They looked to nature and indulged in colorful, often excessive, explorations of human emotions.

As a boarder at the *Collège de Rouen*, a secondary school similar to the one Charles Bovary attends at the beginning of *Madame Bovary*, Flaubert devoured the Romantic writing of Victor Hugo, Jean-Jacques Rousseau, Lord Byron, and Sir Walter Scott (among others), writers who extolled sentiment, feeling, and beauty, often in exotic historical settings. As with other young Frenchmen, Flaubert's turn toward Romanticism led him to reject as coarse, ugly, and unfeeling the middle-class culture that had increased its influence steadily since the end of the Napoleonic era (1815). The very symbol of this culture was the king himself, Louis-Philippe (called the "Citizen King"), who along with his supporters, became the targets of the cartoonist Honoré Daumier (1809–1879) and the novelist Honoré de Balzac (1799–1850). Flaubert and a school friend created their own fictional target, called "le Garçon" (the boy), who represented everything they disliked about middle-class life—its obsession with money and politics, its intellectual pretenses, its vulgarity, and its sexual hypocrisy. Their feelings about this hypocrisy were confirmed somewhat humorously when the respectable vice-principal of the school was discovered in a local brothel.

Flaubert's own attitudes toward love and sexuality, which were to occupy a good part of his later work and correspondence, found their first expression when he was fifteen and fell in love with Elisa Schlésinger, a married woman eleven years his senior. Although she became a friend throughout his later life, Flaubert's obsession with this unattainable "perfect" woman set the tone of later relationships and literary themes. This type of unfulfilled yearning is typical of Romantic love relationships. In Madam Bovary, young Justin, the chemist's assistant, longs for Emma in the same way, and Emma's unfulfilled longing for the perfect love echoes this relationship. Even though Flaubert depicts Emma's desires as the product of an excessive addiction to Romantic ideals, it is possible that he himself was equally their victim. It may also explain in part why Flaubert devoted himself primarily to the search for perfection in his writing rather than in personal relationships. His later relationship with Louise Colet, a poet, confirmed the pattern set by the earlier Schlésinger experience. Colet was also considerably older than Flaubert. Although in love with her, Flaubert carried on their affair primarily through letters; they only saw each other six times during the first two years. In *Madame Bovary*, Emma's romances with Rodolphe and Léon rely heavily on letter-writing.

In 1841, at his father's insistence, Flaubert went to Paris in order to study law, but for two years he led a rather aimless existence, traveling, socializing, and writing. He resumed his friendship with Elisa Schlésinger and became close friends with Maxime DuCamp, a writer and editor. He finished (but did not publish) *November*, a Romantic work about a man's love for a prostitute. Although Flaubert would eventually create a more objective and realistic style, this early novel was typical of the emotional intensity of Romantic literature.

Though he finally began to study law in 1843, he hated every moment of it and felt tremendous stress, possibly the result of a conflict between his literary interests and the pressure to learn a respectable profession. In January 1844, while returning to Rouen for a vacation with his family, the twenty-two-year-old Flaubert suffered a seizure that marked the beginning of a lifelong nervous disorder. On his parents' advice, he gave up the study of law and settled in at the family estate in Croisset, which would become his permanent home. Flaubert became very familiar with provincial living and would draw on this to describe the small, boring towns of Tostes and Yonville in *Madame Bovary*.

Though solitary, Flaubert traveled and kept the apartment in Paris. But when his father and sister died within a few months of one another in 1846, his hostility toward the world intensified and he became even more of a loner. He eventually became known as the "hermit of Croisset."

Avoiding interruptions, he started work on a long historical novel, *The Temptation of Saint Anthony*. His style, marked by attention to detail and tightness of construction, began to take shape. Over the next few years he would become a perfectionist, spending days writing and rewriting a single page, researching his material, or searching tirelessly for the famous *mot juste,* the "exact word." This belief in the precision of language would become a permanent obsession and would characterize his style more than any other technique or device. In *Madame Bovary*, Emma's search for the perfect romance might be said to parallel Flaubert's quest for the *mot juste*.

After spending three years on *Saint Anthony*, Flaubert was shocked that his close friends didn't like it. They suggested he tackle a more realistic subject from daily life that would take him farther beyond his Romantic roots. He shelved the book and went to the Middle East, a setting that was hardly likely to suppress his Romantic tendencies. Ironically, however, the book that he began upon his return was based not on the attractions of exotic locales, but on the everyday life he knew so well.

Madame Bovary parallels the true story of Eugène Delamare, a former student of Flaubert's father who had practiced medicine as an army officer and had married an older woman. After her death, he married a young woman named Delphine Couturier and took up residence in the town of Ry, not far from Rouen. Delphine was unfaithful to him, ran up many debts without his knowledge, then died, leaving him with a young daughter—all of which Emma does in *Madame Bovary*. After a few months, Eugène, like Emma's husband Charles, died in despair.

Flaubert insisted that *Madame Bovary* was entirely fictitious, and when asked about Emma's identity, he would argue, "Madame Bovary, c'est moi" ("**I** am Madame Bovary," or "Madame Bovary is **my** creation"). His intention was to create a type of character, not a specific individual, and he claimed that Emma was "suffering and weeping at this very moment in twenty villages in France"— that is, there were women everywhere in France who were stifled and bored like Emma.

The writing of *Madame Bovary* dominated Flaubert's life from 1851 to 1856. On completing the novel, he made no effort to publish it. But at his friends' insistence, he sent it to the prestigious *Revue de Paris*, which published *Madame Bovary* in installments in 1857. The editors suggested he cut certain "offensive" passages, but the author refused. He might have reacted differently if he had known what lay ahead. Both Flaubert and his publishers were thrown into court on grounds that the novel was morally and religiously offensive to the public. Ironically, when the defendants won their case, *Madame Bovary* became a national bestseller.

The book was also recognized as marking a turning point in the history of the novel. The combination of realistic detail, objective narrative technique, harmony of structure, and language chosen to reflect the characters' personalities created a realistic, yet beautiful, picture for the reader. Drawing on both the Romantic emphasis on inner feelings and the Realist's concern for truth, *Madame Bovary* serves as a bridge between Romanticism and the modern novel.

In Flaubert's next book, *Salammbô* (1862), he returned to an exotic setting and attempted to recreate the civilization of ancient Carthage. In the mid-1860s, he began his most autobiographical novel, *Sentimental Education*, which centered on Frédéric Moreau's failure in an impossible love affair. During this period, he went back to *The Temptation of Saint Anthony*, but his solitude was interrupted by the Franco-Prussian War (1870–71). After the war, Flaubert finally finished *Saint Anthony* (1874) and in 1877 published a group of three short stories (*Trois Contes*). In May 1880, while hard at work on his comic novel *Bouvard and Pécuchet*, Flaubert collapsed and died.

Readers note that few outward events of importance occur in *Madame Bovary*, and the same can be said of Flaubert's life. His concentration on the inner lives of his characters—their memories, dreams, and fantasies—might be said to reflect his own obsessions with love, sexuality, and art. The next generation of French novelists—Emile Zola, Alphonse Daudet, and Guy de Maupassant—considered themselves disciples of this man who has been called "the novelist's novelist." Shortly afterward, in the early twentieth century, the innovative work of the French writer Marcel Proust and the Irish writer James Joyce would be deeply influenced and inspired by Flaubert's techniques of depicting the realities of inner experience.

THE NOVEL

The Plot

It's 1830 and fifteen-year-old Charles Bovary is about to enter a new school in the French city of Rouen. The son of a doting mother and a strict father, he has no idea what he wants to do with his life. Urged on by his mother, he eventually enters medical school, passes the exam on his second try, and establishes a practice in the small town of Tostes. His mother arranges a marriage for him with Héloïse Dubuc, an ugly widow with a modest dowry.

Charles is a hard-working doctor who enjoys a good reputation among the people of Tostes. One night he's called to set the broken leg of Monsieur Rouault at a nearby farm. He meets Emma Rouault, the daughter of the farm owner, and is captivated by her. Héloïse is jealous, but after she dies of a stroke, Charles asks Emma to marry him.

After a big wedding, Charles and Emma return to Tostes. Charles is infatuated with his young wife, who is desperate to experience the passionate love she has read about in romantic novels during her years as a convent student. She has an image of what an ideal marriage should be, but neither Charles nor her life in Tostes lives up to this expectation.

When Emma and Charles are invited to a ball at La Vaubyessard, the estate of a marquis, Emma experiences the kind of life she feels she was born for. This one night—when she dances with a Viscount and mingles with the rich—leaves a lasting impression on her and makes her even more restless with her life at Tostes. As her unhappiness increases, she grows ill. Charles, in consultation with another doctor, decides that a change of scenery might be good for her. By the time they are ready to move to the town of Yonville to start life anew, Emma discovers that she is pregnant.

Yonville isn't much different from Tostes. The only diversion for Emma is Léon Dupuis, a notary's clerk who shares her interest in art and literature.

When Emma gives birth to a daughter, Berthe, it's another disappointment since she was hoping for a boy. In order to compensate for the monotony of her life in Yonville, Emma borrows money from Lheureux, a dry-goods merchant, and treats herself to luxurious items that she feels she deserves.

As time passes, Emma becomes more miserable. Emma and Léon realize that they're in love, but neither is ready for an affair. Finally, Léon moves to Paris, leaving Emma even more unhappy than before.

Rodolphe Boulanger consults Charles over a minor ailment and is sexually attracted to Emma. Deciding that it would be fun to add her to his list of conquests, he makes plans to seduce her. He succeeds, and they become lovers. Every morning Emma rushes to Rodolphe's estate where they make love passionately. Some evenings, after Charles goes to sleep, they meet on a bench in the garden in front of Emma's house. Emma is satisfied for a while, but when Rodolphe begins to take her for granted, she turns back to Charles for satisfaction.

Wishing he would do something to make her proud of him, she encourages Charles to perform an experimental operation on Hippolyte, the stable-boy. The operation turns out to be a disaster and another doctor is called in to amputate Hippolyte's leg.

Her husband's failure makes Emma despise him even more. It rekindles her love for Rodolphe whom she asks to take her away from Yonville. For Rodolphe, however, the novelty of the conquest has worn off and he ends the affair. Emma sinks into a depression and stays in bed for two months. When she recovers, Charles takes her to the opera in Rouen, where they happen to meet Léon. After the opera, Charles goes back to Yonville, but Emma stays an extra day and Léon seduces her.

Emma tries to cover up her affair with Léon by telling Charles that she's going to Rouen to take piano lessons. Once a week, she meets Léon in a hotel room. Meanwhile, her debts to Lheureux are mounting, and she's forced to borrow more money in order to repay him.

One day, Lheureux tells her that unless she pays him 8000 francs, all her property will be seized. Desperately, Emma attempts to raise the money, but no one will help her—not even Léon. Emma is slowly losing her mind and can see no solution but to take her own life. She persuades a young pharmacist's assistant who is secretly in love with her to give her a supply of arsenic. Emma swallows the arsenic, writes Charles a letter of explanation, and dies. Charles dies of a broken heart sometime later, and Berthe goes to live with an aunt who sends her to do menial work in a cotton mill.

The Characters

Emma Bovary

Emma Bovary is one of the most interesting women characters of world literature. But most readers agree that her character can be interpreted in many different ways. One of the major challenges of *Madame Bovary* is to figure out what makes her tick.

During Emma's youth in the early nineteenth century, the literary and artistic movement of Romanticism was in full swing. Romantic novels were the rage, and young girls everywhere read about romantic heroines being swept off their feet by dashing young heroes who carried them away to imaginary lands of love. (Romance novels have made a comeback today, and when you see the rows of them in bookstores, you get an idea of their popularity in Emma's time.)

Flaubert loathed the romantic novels which had fed Emma, because their characters indulged in emotional excesses and behaved idiotically. He knew that the women of his time would recognize themselves in Emma, so he used his character as an example of what can result from such excesses.

Since Emma grew up on an isolated farm with few friends, she began life as a lonely child. Then, upon entering the Catholic convent school, she was completely shut off from the external world and turned inward for excitement. During this time, she read dozens of romance novels and formed an image of the "perfect" lover, who would be strong, handsome, athletic, and artistic. Despite her fantasies of this ideal lover, Emma would be happy only in her dreams. Her pleasure lay in the dreaming, not in the reality of having a lover. One of

Flaubert's reasons for creating Emma Bovary is to show the wreckage that such dreams can bring when the person tries to impose these dreams on reality. When a character like Emma despises the life around her and tries to live her life as she fantasizes it "should" be, the process can destroy both her and her family. At the end of the novel, not only do Emma and Charles die, but their daughter is condemned to a life in the factories.

Yet there is a difference between Emma Bovary—a woman of romance—and the romantic heroines of the novels. The romantic heroines' lives were rigidly structured, whereas Emma rather naïvely follows her instincts. The romantic heroines were a swooning, passive lot, while Emma is an aggressive, energetic woman. If the romantic heroines give gifts to their lovers, Emma does this because she thinks one "must" do it, not because she enjoys it. Much of Emma's sexual education came from the romantic novels, and you've probably noticed how difficult it is to change the ideas you were taught in childhood.

Emma's fantasies are based on the double illusion of time and space. On the one hand, she believes that things will get better as time progresses (illusion of time), and on the other she concludes that her boring existence will improve once she reaches the greener pastures of the good life (illusion of space). Neither of these dreams comes true. Clearly her life falls apart instead of improving, and the "green pastures" seem to get browner.

Some readers believe Emma is more intellectual than emotional—a sensual woman, not a passionate one. They claim that she is guided more by imagination than by physical urges, and that she seems more interested in the *idea* of having a lover than in actually having one. Emma is not a simple woman. On the contrary, there is something extraordinary and rare about her. Whenever Flaubert describes her sensuality, he does so in an almost delicate, religious style. Yet apart from Emma's romantic inclinations, some readers consider her essentially mediocre. She is incapable of understanding things she hasn't experienced, and resembles her Norman peasant ancestors, known for their callous insensitivity. Though she aspires to a life of romance, she is rooted in middle-class materialism and surrounds herself with "objects." Some would say that the struggle between the two is what finally kills Emma Bovary.

Charles

Charles is portrayed as a dull country doctor whom most readers regard as a fool. He is vulgar, primitive, and almost entirely without passion—like a docile animal who wallows in monotony. His devotion to Emma is as blind as a sheep's, and he contributes almost nothing to her life. He has no original ideas, bungles an attempt at curing a clubfoot, and hasn't the slightest notion that he is being victimized by Emma (adultery), Lheureux (debts), and the law (repossession of property). In fact, this sleepy, awkward man has an almost total absence of character. Some readers consider him a "nothing" who merely exists.

At the beginning of the novel, Charles is a schoolboy tied to his mother's apron strings, too timid to assert himself. It's only with the greatest effort that he's able to pass his medical college exams. After graduation, his mother secures a job for him in Tostes, then arranges his marriage. Do you have the feeling that he has no idea what he wants to do and would just as soon have his mother make all his decisions for him?

His marriage enables him to cut loose from his mother, and everything that happens to Charles from this point on results from his decision to marry Emma. Soon after their marriage, Emma sees him as a burden. Some readers, however, see him as a faithful, loving, and forgiving man whose devotion to Emma is a sign of strength. His honesty and hard work also stand out among the number of unscrupulous characters that people Yonville. As you read the novel, ask yourself whether you sympathize with him, respect him, or judge him to be an imbecile for whom "ignorance is bliss."

Léon Dupuis

Léon, a law clerk in a notary's office, meets Emma on her first night in Yonville. He is certainly physically superior to Charles, with ideas that are somewhat fresher. Drawn together by their common interest in music, art, and fashion, he and Emma fall in love. Though Léon is too passive and inexperienced to seduce her physically—and Emma isn't ready for an affair—he does seduce her intellectually and lays the groundwork for their future involvement.

Three years later, when they meet again at the Rouen opera house, Léon has gained experience with the world and women. Acting like most young men of his time, Léon succumbs to Emma, and they begin to meet once a week in a hotel room at Rouen.

Soon after their affair begins, however, Léon seems overpowered by Emma. It's as if their roles have been reversed, with Léon becoming Emma's mistress. Ultimately, she is too much for him. Besides, having an affair with a married woman conflicts with his essentially middle-class values.

If there are two Léons—the naïve youth in Yonville and the sophisticate in Rouen—do you think they are essentially the same or different? Do you agree with Emma's final judgment of him as being "incapable of heroism, weak, banal, softer than a woman, and also stingy"?

Rodolphe

Rodolphe, Emma's first real lover, is a cold seducer with no conscience. He has successfully used the same seductive approach dozens of times, and Emma falls for it no less than his previous conquests. Rodolphe is to Emma's love life what Lheureux is to her financial affairs. He is a vulture who preys on her weakness and exploits her to his own advantage.

To his credit, Rodolphe occasionally seems like the only character who understands Emma's state of mind. Unlike Léon, he's had extensive experience with women and quickly assesses Emma as being bored with her life. He begins plotting her seduction from the moment he sees her and, like a hunter, will chase Emma until he has no further use for her. For Rodolphe—who is dashing and wealthy, but not particularly talented—the conquest means everything. In this way, he is something of a Don Juan figure who enjoys the seductive process more than the end result. He even keeps a box of mementos from old lovers, to which he adds Emma's letters when their affair is over.

Not long after the affair begins, Rodolphe wonders how he'll escape from it. True to the spirit of Don Juan, his treatment of Emma proves to be inhuman—as inhuman as Emma's treatment of

Charles. Emma's blindness to Rodolphe's nature is characteristic of her devotion to dreams at the expense of reality.

Homais

The Yonville pharmacist (apothecary) loves to hear the sound of his own voice and will talk, with assumed authority, about almost any subject. Though merely a pharmacist, he holds court like a master physician for people who come from all over to benefit from his medical "expertise." He is an immensely powerful and prosperous figure in Yonville who, though not a physician, has more patients than any doctor in the area. While busying himself with everything and intruding in every imaginable matter, Homais considers himself the resident intellectual of Yonville—and in this respect Flaubert paints him as a fool. His conversation, though forceful and often stylish, is filled with commonplace clichés and lies. He says whatever is necessary to portray Yonville in a good light or to convince an audience that his opinion is correct.

Homais represents Flaubert's attack on the new middle-class man, the rising bourgeois who has true faith only in materialistic pursuits, which he covers with the progressive-sounding jargon of scientific ideas. It's he who recklessly encourages Charles to perform the clubfoot operation, hoping that it will bring publicity and money to Yonville—and to himself. Yet he's too frightened to witness or help with the surgery. When the operation proves to be a failure, Homais cowardly refuses to take responsibility for suggesting it.

The turning point in Homais' career is his campaign to have the blind beggar removed from the

Yonville-Rouen road. Ironically, Homais' success at having the beggar sent to an asylum is Flaubert's way of ridiculing the pharmacist's smug self-importance. What's more, Homais' success in receiving the prestigious national decoration of the Legion of Honor indicates Flaubert's pessimistic attitude about the direction in which his society was headed. You may disagree with Flaubert's position, however, especially if you see Homais as a vital force in helping society move forward. After all, progress depends on money and scientific discoveries. What is your assessment of the pharmacist?

Lheureux

The drygoods (household items) merchant and money lender of Yonville is as much a seducer as either Rodolphe or Léon. He lies to Emma and takes advantage of her inexperience with financial matters by enticing her with luxurious items. In Lheureux, Flaubert has created a character who reveals middle-class society in all its vulgarity.

By the time he enters the novel, you realize that surface impressions are not reliable. A cruel monster lurks beneath Lheureux's gentle facade. Not only does he consciously get Emma over her head in debt, but he also attempts to come between Emma and Charles by encouraging Emma to have the power of attorney over Charles' financial affairs. When he sees Léon and Emma together, he uses this information to blackmail her. And when Emma comes to see him one last time, hoping that he'll do something to help her out of her financial difficulties, he slams the door in her face. He's used

her, milked her dry, and is completely uncon-
cerned about her fall.

Father Bournisien

The town priest of Yonville, Father Bournisien has
a one-dimensional sense of the needs of his pa-
rishioners. When Emma goes to him, desperate for
help, he can barely understand what she's saying.
He insensitively interrupts her plea for help by telling her that he just cured a sick cow. Bournisien
represents the corruption of religious values in
middle-class society, and in this sense he resembles Homais, with whom he has hilarious argu-
ments.

Binet

The tax-collector of Yonville, Binet is the fourth—
and dullest—of the middle-class types whom
Flaubert portrays. His main occupation is to turn
out napkin rings on his lathe, a meaningless occupation since he never uses them for anything.
They just pile up around his house. Flaubert uses
the background noise of Binet's lathe, however, to
symbolize the meaninglessness of middle-class life.
Its droning sound can be heard when Emma receives the letter from Rodolphe that ends their affair, a signal of the monotonous future that looms
ahead.

Madame Bovary, Senior

She has suffered for many years because of her
husband's infidelities and alcoholism and she takes
her frustrations out on her son, trying to guide and
dominate his life. At first, she arranges his marriage to Héloïse Dubuc, but when Héloïse dies and
Charles marries Emma, her power over Charles
fades. Every time she visits the Bovary household,

she and Emma argue, forcing Charles to take sides. Eventually he sides with his wife, and Madame Bovary, Senior, is driven from the picture.

Charles Bovary, Senior

After he's forced to leave his position as a doctor's assistant in the army, he retires to the country with his wife and son. An unfaithful husband and an alcoholic, he raises Charles strictly, but has no real love for him.

Justin

Homais' nephew, Justin is also his assistant at the pharmacy. Justin is the same age—fifteen or sixteen—as Charles was at the start of the novel. Like Charles, he genuinely loves Emma, and is the only other character in the book who sincerely mourns her death. His role is both tragic and ironic, since it's Justin who shows Emma where to find the arsenic.

Félicité

As Emma's maid, Félicité is probably aware of her mistress' infidelities. After Emma dies, she flees Charles' house with her lover and most of Emma's wardrobe.

Doctor Canivet

Canivet is a doctor from a nearby town whom Charles consults during the operation on the stable boy's clubfoot. Canivet later appears with Doctor Larivière and tries to save Emma's life. He's only slightly more competent than Charles himself, but nonetheless treats Charles as an inferior.

Doctor Larivière

A doctor of great reputation, his character was probably modeled after Flaubert's father. He arrives in Yonville when Emma is dying, but is too late to save her. Though he appears only briefly at the end of the novel, he's one of the few characters with integrity.

Monsieur Rouault

Rouault, Emma's father, is genuinely affected by the death of his wife. A sentimental man, he sends the Bovarys a turkey every year to mark the anniversary of their meeting. At the end, he's too upset by his daughter's death to see his granddaughter, Berthe.

Berthe

Charles and Emma's daughter is left in her aunt's care when her parents die. The aunt eventually puts Berthe to work in a cotton mill to earn her living.

Hippolyte

The stable boy at the Lion d'Or, he allows Charles to perform an experimental operation on his clubfoot. As a result of the disastrous operation, his leg must be amputated.

Other Elements

SETTING

Both Tostes and Yonville, where the main action of *Madame Bovary* takes place, are fictitious names of small towns in the Normandy region of northwest France. Both towns were invented by Flaubert, though many readers assume that Yonville was modeled after the town of Ry, where an actual scandal similar to the story of Emma and Charles had taken place. Originally Flaubert had subtitled the novel "Scenes From Provincial Life" to emphasize the importance of the setting as a commentary on French small-town life in the mid-nineteenth century.

Flaubert describes the town of Yonville in great detail, from the "straight street lined with young aspens" to "the emaciated pear trees pressed up against the plastered walls of the houses." It has only a single main street which is lined with stores. Nothing ever changes in this town or in its surrounding landscape that is as flat and monotonous as the lives of its inhabitants. The farmers continually plow their fields, whether the land is fertile or not. Note especially Flaubert's description of the town cemetery (Part Two, Chapter 1).

Flaubert sets a good portion of Part Three in Rouen, the city of his birth. In his day, Rouen, the capital of Normandy, was the third largest city in France, known mostly for its medieval architecture and especially for the Cathedral where Leon and Emma begin their affair. In *Madame Bovary* the shift from town to city is important to the relatively unsophisticated residents of Yonville. For Homais, a trip to Rouen is a special occasion. During his visit, he makes Leon take him on a tour of the restaurants and cafés, acting like a typical sightseer. On the other hand, you get the impression that Charles prefers small-town life. When he goes to Rouen to buy tickets for the opera, he might as well be in a foreign country. For Emma, city life presents the perfect remedy for her boredom, almost a dream come true. The crowded streets provide her with enough excitement to blot out, at least momentarily, her usual morbid thoughts. For Emma, Rouen represents another imagined escape route from everyday reality. Similarly, Paris, the glittering city that seems paradise to Emma, serves as the backdrop to many of her fantasies.

THEMES

The following are themes of *Madame Bovary*.

1. BLINDNESS

The blind beggar whose melancholy song Emma hears just before she dies symbolizes the lack of insight that characterizes the main figures in *Madame Bovary*. Charles might also be thought of as blind—to Emma's unhappiness and to her unfaithfulness. Even when he discovers Rodolphe's and Léon's letters at the end of the novel, he still refuses to accept the truth. For her part, Emma is unable to see through either her own self-deceiving view of life or the deceptions of others. She idealizes her lovers and is fooled by both the false ideas of Homais and the unscrupulous practices of Lheureux.

2. INADEQUACY AND FAILURE

Madame Bovary is a record of Emma's failure to find a life which corresponds to the vague, romantic notions which she has read about. Each failure leads to another attempt at self-fulfillment. She accepts Charles' marriage proposal, thinking that a life with him will solve the boredom of life on her father's farm. But Charles becomes the symbol of everything inadequate or wrong with her life. The failure of the clubfoot operation represents both Emma's thwarted expectations and Charles' mediocrity.

3. HUMAN INSENSITIVITY

Most of the relationships in *Madame Bovary* are marked by an extreme lack of sensitivity and love.

tor and that Flaubert spent much of his childhood in a hospital environment. The precision with which Flaubert brings his characters and their surroundings to life in many ways resembles the work of a scientist. And like a careful scientist, he tries to stick to the objective, concrete facts about his characters in their setting that will reveal their essence.

In a letter written while he was working on *Madame Bovary*, he referred to the book as "an exercise in style." He thought the actual *subjects* he was writing about—the people, the story, the places—were unimportant and that the only way to redeem the book was by making it into a great work of art. He did this by trying to bridge the gap between form and content, by attempting to make the words he used merge with the things he was describing. To do this, he searched almost fanatically for the "mot juste," the uniquely perfect word. That is, every word had to be exactly right to reveal the essence of the thing being described. To create a book in this way is a laborious, painstaking job, and it's no wonder it took Flaubert five years to finish *Madame Bovary*.

Flaubert uses description of physical things— clothes, food, buildings, nature, carriage rides—as another dimension of his story. In many novels, descriptive passages serve as intermissions in the plot, but in *Madame Bovary* they're an integral part of the story. For example, Flaubert's description of Charles' cap in the opening scene tells you as much about its owner as you might get in several pages of character analysis. In a similar vein, Flaubert conveys the aimlessness of Emma's affair with Léon by taking you on an endless cab ride through the streets of Rouen. The long, winding sentences parallel the drawn-out nature of the trip. The description of Rouen Cathedral at the beginning of Part Three is another example of a passage rich with meaning. And, the many descriptions of food throughout *Madame Bovary* often are reminders of lust. For example, notice the elaborately detailed description of the feast at Emma and Charles' wedding, where "big dishes of yellow custard, on whose smooth surface the newlyweds' initials had been inscribed in arabesques of sugar-coated almonds, quivered whenever the table was given the slightest knock."

Symbolism is an important stylistic device in *Madame Bovary*. Note the frequent use of windows to help create a mood. A closed window might symbolize the reality and monotony of small-town life and of the limitations of marriage, while open windows might symbolize dreams and freedom. Other important symbols are the dried wedding bouquets of both Emma and Charles' first wife, as well as the blind beggar.

Word imagery, also, is important. Flaubert uses many liquid images to convey sensuality, boredom, and even death. The liquids take on various forms from oozing, dripping, and melting to oceans, rivers, tides, torrents, and waves. Emma's passion for Rodolphe is referred to as a "river of milk." His fading love is "the water of a river sinking into its bed." There are many related images of dampness, drowning, and boats.

Flaubert's attention to detail and his reliance on description to tell his story have led to the labeling of his style as realistic, or giving an objective impression of real life. He creates this effect both by using a great number of accurate details as building blocks and by carefully selecting and arranging them into a new reality, the world of *Madame Bovary*. Later in the nineteenth century, writers like Emile Zola and Alphonse Daudet pushed this focus on realistic detail even further by including even the most disgusting aspects of life in their works, usually for the purpose of social criticism.

By selecting and arranging the details, Flaubert hoped to capture the essence of the life he described instead of merely reproducing it. Readers disagree on whether he succeeded. Some see the descriptive passages as plodding and slow, and the accumulation of details as monotonous. As you read such scenes as Emma's wedding in Tostes, the ball at La Vaubyessard, and the agricultural fair in Yonville, you will form your own reactions to Flaubert's realistic style.

Madame Bovary was, of course, written in French. Since Flaubert spent so much time trying to find the precise word for every situation, the book presents a tremendous challenge to the translator. Four widely read English translations are available. Notice how the translators handle the book's opening sentence:

> We were at preparation, when the headmaster came in, followed by a new boy dressed in "civvies" and a school servant carrying a big desk.
>
> *(tr. by Alan Russell)*

> We were studying when the headmaster came in, followed by a new boy, not yet wearing a school uniform, and a monitor carrying a large desk.
>
> *(tr. by Mildred Marmur)*

> We were in the study hall when the headmaster walked in, followed by a new boy not wearing a school uniform, and by a janitor carrying a large desk.
>
> *(tr. by Lowell Bair)*

> We were in study-hall when the headmaster
> entered, followed by a new boy not yet in school
> uniform and by the handyman carrying a large
> desk.
>
> *(tr. by Francis Steegmuller)*

See how the French words "garçon de classe" are rendered as "school servant," "monitor," "janitor," and "handyman" by the translators. (Russell's use of "school servant" and "civvies" indicates that this is a British translation.) Similarly, every page of *Madame Bovary* differs noticeably from one English version to another. While this might occur in translations of other foreign works, it is especially significant for the work of Flaubert with its emphasis on precision of expression. All translators try, in their various ways, to capture the tone and meaning of the original. Your choice of translation will affect your overall impression of the novel. (To fully experience the results of Flaubert's intense devotion to style, the original is the best source.)

This guide is based on the translation by Lowell Bair (Bantam Books, 1959).

POINT OF VIEW

The opening pages of *Madame Bovary* are told from the point of view of one of Charles Bovary's schoolmates in the first person plural ("we"). This "character" disappears midway through the first chapter and the rest of the story is written from the point of view of an omniscient third-person narrator.

Flaubert's aim was to make himself (the writer) disappear from his work, to become, as he said, like "God," who creates but whose creation stands apart without direct evidence of the creator. He also wanted to resemble a scientist who presents his evidence (his characters and their surroundings) in a precise, objective manner—to create an appearance of reality. One of the techniques that Flaubert uses to create the impression of objective reality is the *style indirect libre* (free, indirect style), indirect narrative that makes the narrator seem "absent." For example, instead of saying, "Emma wanted some fruit" or "Emma thought some fruit would be nice," the writer merely says, "Some fruit will be nice." By dropping the real subject of the sentence, Emma, it is implied in an *indirect* way that the idea of eating fruit originated with Emma, and that her direct thoughts are being expressed.

This intermittent use of "absent" narration creates an illusion of objectivity and detachment by pushing the character into the foreground as the narrator recedes into the background. At the same time, it allows an intense close-up focus on the characters and especially on Emma, who is the chief object of the narrative. You will learn about her actions through the traditional third-person approach, but you will also be able better to read her thoughts, feel her feelings, and catch her reactions as a result of the indirect style. Although the focus occasionally shifts to Charles, Léon, Rodolphe or others, Emma's presence remains central.

Despite Flaubert's attempt to distance himself from his characters objectively, his involvement with Emma seems so deep that many readers see her as a "self-portrait" of the author. They say that is why, when asked who Emma was based on, Flaubert usually replied *"Madame Bovary, c'est moi!"* (I am Madame Bovary!).

FORM AND STRUCTURE

Madame Bovary is divided into three sections, each exploring a crucial part of Emma Bovary's life and her three attempts to find romantic fulfillment in three different but neighboring locales.

Part One introduces you to Charles and Emma and describes their early married life in Tostes. Charles is the focus of the first few chapters, and it is through his eyes that Emma is first described. Her past is then revealed (by contrasting her convent experiences with Charles' life in medical school). Emma's hopes that Charles will be the romantic fulfillment of her convent dreams are disappointed. The two contrasting focal events of Part One are the low-class wedding and the aristocratic ball at the château of La Vaubyessard. The ball gives Emma a real taste of the life-style about which she has only dreamed and tempts her to look outside her marriage for happiness.

Part Two details the life of the couple in the dull town of Yonville as Emma embarks on her second attempt to find the romance of her dreams and escape the dreariness of marriage. Flaubert introduces the backdrop of middle-class small-town society against which Emma's story will be played. The agricultural show—with its counterpoint between Emma and Rodolphe's romantic conversation and the mundane details of rural life—is the focal event of this section. Emma's romantic hopes are again frustrated, this time by Rodolphe's eventual rejection. Part Two closes with the introduction of a third and new hope for the future; Emma and Léon (with whom she had been infatuated on first arriving in Yonville) meet again in Rouen.

Part Three centers on Emma's increasing desperation and her love affair with Léon, which is carried on primarily in Rouen. Emma's total rejection of her married life and any notion of respectability leads to her own and her family's ruin. The final rejection of her romantic hopes, in an ugly scene of death by poisoning, contrasts pointedly with the description, early in Part Three, of Emma and Léon's meeting in the Rouen Cathedral. The two focal points of this section are Emma's flights into Rouen for romance and her steady decline into debt through her irresponsible financial dealings with the unscrupulous merchant Lheureux. *Madame Bovary* closes, as it had opened, with Charles, first with his hopes and last with his despair and death.

In this three-part structure, centered on Emma's repeated attempts to find in reality the fulfillment of her chronic, romantic dreaming, the action is less concerned with the chronological advancement of events than with presenting each part as an "act" complete with its own setting and set of relationships. Within these acts are a succession of scenes, many of which reverberate against one another like the themes in a piece of music. And, across the scenes are repeated images and symbols, as well as the technique of "double action" that creates a counterpoint of parallel, contrasting actions within the same scene.

Almost every page of *Madame Bovary* contains something—a word, description, action, memory, piece of clothing, or object—that relates it to another part of the book. The scenes at Emma's wedding are meant to be compared to the ball at La Vaubyessard. The seduction of Emma by Ro-

dolphe parallels her seduction by Léon. The agricultural fair and the Bovarys' arrival at the Lion
d'Or inn both contain strands of contrasting conversations and situations that act as counterpoint
in the general orchestration of the scene. The
charred black paper "butterflies" that float from
Emma's burning wedding bouquet are recalled later
on by the white paper "butterflies" that Emma lets
fly from the carriage during the ride when she gives
herself to Léon.

Some readers compare *Madame Bovary* to the
carefully constructed edifice of an architect or engineer; some compare it to a painting; others see
it as a symphony, and still others think it resembles a play. Whichever analogy you think most
appropriate, you will find it hard to ignore the
way almost all the elements of the novel fit together. You may find that Flaubert's attention to
structure and detail detracts from the story and
makes it move too slowly. You may think everything a bit too controlled to fully convey the passion and reality of the characters. You may feel
that the devotion to accurate description creates
monotony. But you cannot fail to admire the way
Flaubert has put together the pieces of an entire
society over a span of almost twenty years and at
the same time painted a complex inner portrait of
an unforgettable woman.

Compared with other nineteenth-century novels, *Madame Bovary* contains relatively little action.
A good deal of the activity takes place in the minds
of the characters. As you read, note the way Flaubert shifts back and forth between external reality
(what the characters do and say) and internal reality (their memories and dreams). The dreams are,

in fact, an important part of the "action" in the book.

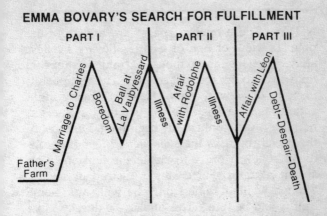

EMMA BOVARY'S SEARCH FOR FULFILLMENT

The Story
PART I
CHAPTER 1

The book opens with a glimpse of Charles Bovary as a shy fifteen-year-old on his first day at a new school. It's an experience you can probably identify with—being in a new place for the first time, aware that everyone is watching and waiting to see what you're like. Charles' clothes are too tight for him, and he's too nervous even to hang up his cap like his fellow students. When the teacher asks him his name, he can barely open his mouth, and in his confusion he finally shouts out "Charbovari" (a country hick's way of saying Charles Bovary). You also see that his attempt to be a serious student saves him from being placed in a lower grade, even though he doesn't seem particularly intelligent.

NOTE: These opening pages are told from the point of view of one of Charles Bovary's fellow students. This anonymous narrator disappears midway through the first chapter. The abrupt shift in point of view is one of Flaubert's many innovations as a novelist. He will use this first-person narrator ("we") only at the beginning. For most of the novel, he uses the *style indirect libre* (free, indirect style) in order to create the illusion of an absent narrator. For example, instead of saying, "Emma wanted some fruit," he will say, "Some fruit would be nice." This implies—indirectly—that the idea of eating fruit originated with Emma, not with Flaubert. This "absent" narrator creates an illusion of objectivity and detachment. You will come across many examples of this style as you read.

In a flashback, you learn about Charles' childhood and the relationship between his parents. His father had begun his career as an army doctor but was involved in a scandal and was dismissed. He married Charles' mother for her money, but ended up squandering most of it on women and alcohol. After their money had run out, the couple moved to a small farm where they tried, with little success, to settle down peacefully.

At first, Charles' mother tolerated her husband's affairs, but after a few years she became bitter and disillusioned. When Charles was born, she focused her hopes on him and fantasized that he'd become a successful lawyer or engineer. Charles' youth was ultimately dominated by his mother— a foreshadowing of what his marriages to Héloïse and Emma would be like.

NOTE: Provincial setting   Notice that Flaubert gives you many details about the rural setting n which *Madame Bovary* takes place. Charles grows up in the country, then attends secondary school in Rouen, the main city of the province of Normandy to the northwest of Paris. The lower middle-class characters (members of the *petit* [small] bourgeoisie) represent what Flaubert detested most in life: smugness, vulgarity, greed, and ignorance. They aspired to money, power, and respectability—not to art or beauty.

After attending the lycée (high school) in Rouen— where the novel begins—Charles enrolls in medical school. He is a mediocre student and is overwhelmed by the amount of work required of him. Not surprisingly, he fails his final exams, but his mother blames this on the examiner and refuses to face up to her son's inadequacies. Charles returns to medical school, works harder, and finally manages to pass the tests.

His mother finds him a position as a doctor in the town of Tostes. She also finds him a wife—the ugly, middle-aged widow, Héloïse Dubuc, whose main asset is her small yearly income. Héloïse is a dominating shrew—much like Charles' mother— who forces her tastes on her young husband. Because of her jealousy, she spies on him when women patients come to his office.

NOTE: Charles Bovary Charles is a weak-willed person who's easily controlled by other people, especially women. He's not very bright and must work hard at everything in order to succeed. He seems to have no particular interest in medicine, yet he becomes a doctor—no doubt to please his mother. Similarly, he has little feeling for Héloïse, yet marries her anyway. Would you marry someone you didn't love in order to please your parents? Or would you enter a career just because someone else wanted it for you? Since Charles gives in on both accounts, what conclusions can you draw about his character?

CHAPTER 2

In the middle of the night, a messenger arrives at Charles' house with the news that a nearby farmer, Monsieur Rouault, has broken his leg. Héloïse thinks it's too dangerous to travel by night, so Charles sets out at dawn on the fifteen-mile trip. Half-asleep, he recalls his life as a student and compares it to his present life as a doctor and married man.

NOTE: Interior monologue In Flaubert's work, it is usual to see memories of objects and people from the distant past interacting with events of the present. Flaubert was one of the first novelists who tried to show how people think—the way one thought connects with another. This analysis of the mental process had an important influence on many twentieth-century writers, especially Marcel Proust and James Joyce, who both developed further the technique known as interior monologue or stream of consciousness. As mentioned earlier, Flaubert uses an indirect narrative approach to take you inside the minds of his characters. He describes their thoughts and reactions without directly stating who is doing the thinking or reacting, so that it seems as if the character has replaced the narrator. This is the process that occurs as Charles travels to the farm. From what you already know about him, do you think he would express his thoughts in the same language if he was reminiscing directly in the first person?

Arriving at the farm—called Les Bertaux—Charles is met by Rouault's beautiful young daughter, Emma. He sets Rouault's leg without any problems, and notices Emma's hands as she helps him with the bandages. Her eyes look straight at him "with naïve boldness," and Charles is struck by her elegance.

Over the next few months, Charles visits the Rouault household regularly, even though Monsieur Rouault is fully recovered. Héloïse, suspicious about Charles' new happiness, inquires about Rouault's daughter. Consumed by jealousy, she makes her husband promise never to visit the farm again. But this backfires on her since Charles quickly becomes aware of his infatuation.

NOTE: Flaubert introduces you to Emma but doesn't tell you much about her. What you know is filtered through the impressions of Charles and Héloïse. By introducing the sensual Emma into Charles' dull world, Flaubert sets up one of the many contrasts that will echo and reverberate throughout *Madame Bovary*. Bovary's early dreams of romance with Emma will be echoed by her dreams of a romantic marriage with him. Also, the contrast between the shrewish Héloïse and Emma will be recalled when Emma replaces Héloïse and turns out to be different from this initial impression she makes both on you and on Charles. As you read, notice Flaubert's skill in presenting Emma. With each chapter, you will learn a little more, and the different aspects of her character will gradually come together into a complete portrait.

Later that spring, the notary who had handled Héloïse's estate embezzles the remainder of her money. Charles' parents are outraged since Héloïse's main attraction was her modest income. A violent quarrel takes place between Charles' parents and his wife, and a week later, Héloïse collapses and dies suddenly in the front yard.

CHAPTER 3

Monsieur Rouault consoles Charles by describing his own feelings of despair at the loss of his wife. He advises Charles to continue visiting Les Bertaux. But Charles isn't really suffering. Though he occasionally thinks about Héloïse, he has begun to enjoy a feeling of freedom—the first in his life since he is no longer controlled by a domineering woman.

One afternoon Charles arrives at the farm and finds Emma alone in the kitchen. The shutters are closed, and he watches as she tilts a glass of liqueur to her lips. He dwells on the sensual way in which she licks the bottom of the empty glass. Later, as he returns home, Charles tries to imagine how it would feel to be married to someone like Emma. It is not long before he realizes that he is falling in love with her.

NOTE: Window symbolism   Flaubert uses windows as a symbol of freedom or restraint, depending on whether they are open or closed. When Charles visits Emma, she is seated in the kitchen with the shutters closed. She's shut in and stifled with her monotonous country life. When Charles gets up in the middle of the night—too excited by his thoughts of Emma to fall asleep—he sits by the open window and watches the stars, an indication of the promise that his dreams open up for him. As you read, notice how Flaubert uses windows to reflect the emotional states of his characters.

Since Charles has become fond of Emma and since she is of no use around the farm, Rouault sees no reason why she should not marry the young doctor. Preparations for the marriage will be made during the winter, and the ceremony will take place in the spring. Inspired by her romantic novels, Emma would like to marry at midnight, by torchlight, but her father insists on a traditional country wedding feast, which will last three days.

NOTE: Emma's character   What do you know of Emma's character at this point? From her father you learn that she's too clever to spend her life on a farm. She has an interest in music, but no par-

ticular talent. It is suggested that she has a romantic nature; both her sensuality and tastes (for a
torchlit wedding) are placed into contrast with her
dull surroundings. After reading the next three
chapters, compare the Emma you will know then
with the young girl about to marry. What hints
has Flaubert already given to prepare you for the
Madame Bovary you will get to know? Whose view
of Emma have you been seeing up to this point?
Watch, as you read, to see when and how this
early portrait changes.

CHAPTER 4

The guests arrive at Charles and Emma's wedding from as far as twenty-five miles away. For a
country wedding, it seems like a lavish affair.
Flaubert's interest in concrete details can be seen
in his intricate descriptions of the women in their
city-style dresses, the men in tail coats, frock coats,
and so on. Everyone has fun except for Charles'
mother, who is angry about not being included in
the wedding preparations. After two days of wedding parties, the young couple returns to Tostes.

NOTE: Realism Realism is often defined as an
artistic representation that is visually accurate.
Though Flaubert hated the term—and once de-
clared that "it was in hatred of realism that I un-
dertook this book"—he was a master at describing
things clearly and accurately. His chief goal, however, was not to reproduce a photographically correct picture of life. He wanted to create a beautiful
book (art) out of the trivial, often ugly, lives of

mediocre people in a nondescript section of France. Flaubert rejected Realism as a literary style that reveled in detail for its own sake. But he used detail as the building blocks of his beautiful structure.

In a few paragraphs describing the wedding feast he portrays the spirit of social life in nineteenth-century provincial France. Though you're reading an English translation, see if Flaubert lives up to his ideal that every word must capture the essence of the thing being described. Read closely, for example, the paragraph about food; note the detail with which every aspect of the meal is described. Does the description of the food and other details tell you anything else about the wedding? About the characters? About the social setting?

CHAPTER 5

Charles takes Emma to her new home, and Flaubert describes its contents in detail. To her horror, Emma finds Héloïse's dried wedding bouquet, which Charles had carelessly left in the bedroom. This is the first indication that he will underestimate the intensity of his wife's emotions. After Charles removes this dead symbol of his first marriage that foreshadows the fate of his second, Emma wonders ominously what will become of her own bouquet after she dies. (In Chapter 9 the symbolism of the wedding bouquet will become more clear.)

Emma's disillusionment with Charles begins almost immediately. The feast, the wedding night, and the dead bouquet—everything seems to be going wrong. Her desire to make changes in the household is the first sign of that restlessness and desire for change that characterizes her dream-soaked nature and foreshadows trouble ahead.

Charles is infatuated with his wife and, in typical bourgeois style, sees her as a possession. But he has no curiosity about what's going on beneath the surface, what she's thinking and feeling, and whether she's truly happy. You catch a glimpse of the real Emma for the first time when Flaubert takes you into her mind. She had assumed she was in love with Charles before marrying him, but has not yet begun to experience the "bliss" or "ecstasy" which she has read about in the romantic novels. Love should bring happiness, and because she doesn't feel happy, she wonders if it was a mistake to marry Charles.

CHAPTER 6

Until now, you've mainly seen Emma through the eyes of others. In this chapter, Flaubert breaks into the story of Emma's marriage to take you back to her childhood and adolescence. Do you think this technique of gradually revealing Emma's character is an effective one? Does it make you want to know more about her?

At thirteen, Emma had been sent to a convent school by her father. She took her religious duties seriously, enjoyed the company of the nuns, and studied her catechism diligently. But she was most aroused by the aspects of the convent atmosphere, its perfumed altars, the cool water of the holy-water fonts, and the radiance of the candles. In the sermons, phrases like "heavenly lover" and "eternal wedlock" took on a meaning that was more emotional and erotic than spiritual. As a result, she invented sins so that she could linger close to the priest in the intimacy of the confession booth as long as possible.

NOTE: Keep an eye on the connection between sexual and religious imagery and symbolism. It will play a special role later in the novel when Emma meets Léon in the Cathedral in Rouen. And the convent imagery of mixed sexuality and piety will be recalled in Emma's deathbed scene. The suggestion of a relationship between carnal desire and religion was one of the main reasons that the author and publishers of *Madame Bovary* were prosecuted in the French courts for an "outrage against public morals and religion." They were acquitted but the case caused a public furor.

Once a week an old spinster came to the convent to mend the linen. She let the older girls read the romantic novels that she carried in her pockets, and these books filled Emma's mind with images of lovers meeting their mistresses in lonely country houses. Emma developed a passion for the historical romances of the famous Scottish novelist, Sir Walter Scott. She imagined herself living in an old castle, looking out a window as her lover galloped across the countryside.

NOTE: Romanticism   In *Madame Bovary*, Flaubert attempted to describe Romanticism in its most extreme and degenerate form. He wanted to show how the original idea of Romanticism had been corrupted. As a child, Emma fed her sensitive nature by reading popular novels that were them-

selves a corrupt form of the great Romantic literature of the early nineteenth century. In this chapter,
Emma is portrayed as being hopelessly taken with
romantic notions—a young girl who had read *Paul
and Virginia*, the sentimental novel that was immensely popular in the early nineteenth century.
Her dreamworld merged with the reality of her life
in the convent, and offered her a way of surviving
the monotony of that existence. She identified
strongly with the sentiments of the romantic heroines. But the adult Emma will do something that
these heroines would never have dared to do—
she will seek sexual satisfaction outside her marriage and will indulge her fantasies, despite the
consequences.

At the convent, Emma received news of her
mother's death. This was her first true loss, and
she wept for several days. She consoled herself
with sentimental poetry, feeling that she'd finally
attained the role of the romantic heroine. But after
a while, she became bored with the unhappiness
of such a heroine's life and rebelled against the
strictness of convent life. With that, her father removed her from the school.

NOTE: Do you think Flaubert is being satirical in
his description of Emma's reaction to her mother's
death? In your opinion, does Emma care deeply
about her mother's death? Or does she only be-
have as she believes a romantic heroine would?
What evidence can you find for your opinion?

Back at her father's farm, Emma enjoyed managing the servants but soon grew tired of country life. When Charles arrived on the scene, she realized that there was still something missing in her life. Love and romance were supposed to make one feel ecstatic, yet Emma felt nothing but restlessness and boredom.

CHAPTER 7

Not surprisingly, life in Tostes doesn't measure up to Emma's expectations of the ideal honeymoon. She imagines traveling in the mountains, visiting countries with exotic names, and spending nights in a villa where she and her husband can gaze at the stars, hold each other's hands, and talk about the future. In short, she sees a wide gap between her life with Charles and that of a romantic heroine.

Emma realizes that she can never discuss her yearnings with Charles. He is dull, insensitive, and stupid. His conversation is "as flat as a sidewalk" and he's unaware of life's refinements. So Emma spends her days playing the piano, drawing, and writing letters to Charles' patients who have not paid their bills. Charles idolizes his wife and has no idea that she isn't happy with their life.

NOTE: The gap widens   From now on, the more Charles loves and grows dependent on Emma, the more she will withdraw from him. She does not admire a man who is content with his station in life. She is ambitious, restless, and anxious for perpetual change. Once she achieves a desired goal, she wants to move on to something new. Can you

sympathize with her? Or is this a sign of imma-
turity and a distorted sense of reality? Isn't she
really happiest when longing and suffering?

In an effort to spark romance into their marriage,
Emma recites love poems to Charles in the garden—but to no avail. She begins to doubt Charles'
love for her since he embraces her only at certain
times of the day. Not all men, she concludes, are
like Charles, and perhaps she should have waited
for Mr. Right to come along. She longs for the
passionate and fiery advances of a lover, and wonders what kinds of husbands her former class-
mates have.

Finally, something exciting happens. The Bovarys receive an invitation to a ball at La Vaubyessard, the château of the Marquis d'Andervilliers,
one of Charles' former patients. The couple sets
out for the Marquis' residence in their modest buggy
and arrives at nightfall.

NOTE: Flaubert's Realism Compare the description of La Vaubyessard with that of Emma and
Charles' wedding. This will help you appreciate
Flaubert's realistic, almost scientific, writing style.
The people in these scenes represent two distinctly
different social groups and can be thought of as
specimens being examined under a microscope.

CHAPTER 8

The Marquis greets the Bovarys at the door of
his splendid château, La Vaubyessard. It is filled

with art and expensive furnishings, and the guests are members of the aristocracy. For Emma, being in the company of great wealth is like a dream come true. She drinks champagne and gazes in awe at the pomegranates and pineapples, neither of which she's ever tasted before.

NOTE: Emma thinks that she fits perfectly into these luxurious surroundings. Her observations about the noblemen, in particular, make them seem so desirable and exquisite in comparison to the others. But there is something else about them that Emma may be aware of but doesn't cause her to reflect. They possess "the special brutality that comes from half-easy triumphs which test one's strength and flatter one's vanity—the handling of thoroughbred horses, the pursuit of loose women." This describes fairly well Rodolphe, Emma's first lover, and it foreshadows the nature of their relationship and the way that her romantic conceptions will prevent her from distinguishing between herself and a "loose" woman.

Emma seems embarrassed by the provincial Charles and pushes aside his attempted affections. During the dance, Emma watches a young lady pass an amorous note to a possible suitor. It's like a scene right out of a romantic novel, and she revels in the atmosphere. For a brief moment, time stops and Emma finds her world. At three in the morning, she's still on the dance floor, waltzing with a gentleman known as the Viscount, who spins Emma around dizzily until the hem of her gown catches on his trousers.

Where is Charles all this time? More and more
he fades from the foreground and ceases to interest Emma. By not mentioning Charles, Flaubert
brings a partial death to his character. In Emma's
mind, her new husband is already a thing of the
past.

Charles has spent the night watching people play
whist (a card game) without being able to make
sense of the game. With relief, he climbs into bed,
but Emma stares out the window at the rain.

On returning to Tostes, Emma seethes with anger about her lowly life-style. She is frustrated by
Charles' boorish manner and believes she deserves
better. In a fit of rage, she fires a maid who has
been faithful to Charles. Though Emma tries to
rekindle the memories of the ball at La Vaubyessard, they soon fade into a blur.

NOTE: On Emma   Emma's dreams have—for a
moment—become reality in this chapter. She mingles with aristocrats and carries it off quite well.
Emma possesses the qualities necessary for success in that world, and this is made clear in her
symbolic dance with the Viscount. But a close ex-
amination of this world as described at the ball,
shows that the aristocrats are not really superior
to their middle-class counterparts except for their
surface charm, wealth, and manners. Emma will
find this out through her experience with Rodolphe.

CHAPTER 9

Now that Emma has tasted of her dreamworld,
she finds Tostes unbearable. She has fantasies of

opulent parties attended by nobelmen and aristocrats, and in the process she becomes even more critical of Charles. Having never been to Paris, Emma daydreams about the Viscount and about the excitement of the capital, where everyone is surely in love. She devours travel books and fashion magazines, along with the anti-middle-class novels of Honoré de Balzac and the Romantic works of George Sand, the pseudonym of the famous, flamboyant, and free-living woman writer of the early nineteenth century.

Charles, whose limited vision keeps him from understanding Emma's needs, seems unaware of her state of mind. He subscribes to a medical journal in an effort to keep up with his field. But whenever he begins to read after dinner, he falls asleep within five minutes. Emma stares at him critically from across the room, wishing she'd married someone more exceptional. Ironically, however, the people of Tostes like his attentive bedside manner. Could it be that he has many positive features which neither Emma nor Flaubert want to acknowledge? Would these features (related to his plodding sense of professional duty and perhaps to his basic kindness) be of interest to someone like Emma? One of the questions that *Madame Bovary* brings up in a general way is the bleak picture of human nature that the characters represent. By making Charles fairly decent but horribly mediocre and dull, is Flaubert giving decency a chance?

Emma waits anxiously for a change in her life, but nothing happens. As her unhappiness increases, she stops playing the piano and abandons her sketchbooks and sewing. Even her novels leave her cold. She begins to neglect her household duties and finally gets sick. Charles, not being a particularly good judge of nonphysical illness, assumes that something about the town of Tostes is causing Emma's illness, so he takes her to one of his old medical professors, who recommends a change of scenery.

NOTE: The Romantic "illness" Flaubert explores Emma's state of mind in great detail. This is an important chapter, coming directly after the ball at La Vaubyessard and at the close of Part One. Flaubert demonstrates the influence of emotions on physical health and describes Emma's life almost completely in terms of her dreams and expectations. One of Flaubert's intentions is to depict the extremes of Romanticism and to show how adherence to the ideals of romantic heroines can lead to despair. You might empathize easily with Emma in her boring, rural surroundings. Perhaps you can also identify with her increasing dependence on the world of dreams. The problem with Emma is that her dreams do not nourish happiness; they merely provoke and prolong her unhappiness. Their realization, however, may not be any better than their frustration. It may be that their unattainability is the very cause of their potency.

Charles doesn't want to leave Tostes, but he'll do anything for the sake of Emma's health. He learns that the town of Yonville-l'Abbaye needs a doctor, so he decides to move. What does this self-sacrifice tell you about Charles' character? Do you see it as a weakness or a strength?

While preparing for the move, Emma pricks her

finger on her bridal bouquet. Disgusted, she throws
it into the fire and watches it burn. By the time
they're ready to leave Tostes and start a new life,
Emma discovers that she's pregnant.

NOTE: The symbolic bouquet The description of
the burning bouquet, with its "burnt" berries and
"shriveled" paper "black butterflies," symbolizes
everything that's wrong with Emma's life. It is a
physical reminder of her union with Chalres Bovary. Just as its flowers have withered and died, so
too have Emma's hopes of realizing her dreams in
married life with a country doctor. Her pregnancy
seems, at this low point in Emma's life, just another unpleasant reminder of her ties to the reality
of marriage. The departure for a new town, Yonville-l'Abbaye, and the imminence of a new life
don't seem to hold much attraction for Emma. They
are not the stuff of which her kind of dreams are
made.

PART II
CHAPTER 1

   From his realistic description of Yonville, Flaubert makes it clear that this town is no better than
Tostes. It contains only one street, lined with a few
shops and the only sight that might catch your eye
is Homais' pharmacy, with its colored glass jars in
the front window.

   On the evening of the Bovarys' arrival, they meet
Madame Lefrançois, the proprietor of the Lion d'Or
inn, Homais, the pharmacist (apothecary), Binet,
the tax-collector, and Father Bournisien, the town

priest. Homais and the priest argue about religion. Homais, a rising middle-class citizen, professes to be a free-thinker who believes in his own personal god as opposed to the traditional God of Christianity. In the course of his argument, he attempts to link himself to all the advanced thinkers of his day, a sign that Homais believes in the cult of science and progress.

NOTE: Homais is a caricature of the middle-class individual whom Flaubert despised. Just as the Romanticism which Emma has read about stands for a form of Romanticism fashionable in early nineteenth-century France, so Homais typifies the middle-class mentality of his time and its intellectual pretensions. He's overconfident and filled with a lot of ill-digested knowledge. As you read his speeches, however, ask yourself whether his ideas amount to anything substantial.

You're also introduced to Monsieur Lheureux, the dry goods (household items), merchant who was riding in the same carriage as Charles and Emma. At the same time that Emma gets increasingly involved in romantic adventures, she gets increasingly involved in financial dealings with Lheureux. Her blindness to his unscrupulousness will have dire consequences for her.

CHAPTER 2

The Bovarys—along with their maid, Félicité—descend from the carriage and enter the inn. Across the room, Léon Dupuis, a young clerk in the office of the town notary, watches Emma. Every night Léon arrives at the inn for dinner, hoping he'll meet a traveler with whom he can spend the night talking. In this sense, Léon is very much like Emma, in that he is always waiting for something new and exciting to happen.

During dinner, Homais tries to impress Charles with his knowledge of medicine and science. Léon and Emma strike up a conversation, and it's immediately clear, as they discuss their love for the ocean, mountain scenery, and music that they share the same romantic ideas. During the conversation, Léon rests his foot familiarly on the rung of Emma's chair, and for a moment everyone else in the room fades into the background.

NOTE: The twin conversations of Charles with Homais and Emma with Léon are an example of the counterpoint that Flaubert uses to underscore contrasts. Compare the two conversations. On the one hand, Flaubert makes fun of the shallowness of middle-class knowledge and its devotion to the concrete. On the other, he satirizes the Romantic concern with nature and dramatic situations. The characters are mouthing second-hand ideas rather than expressing themselves.

It's getting late, however, and time for Charles and Emma to go to their new home, which is only about fifty yards from the inn. As Emma lies in bed that night, she remembers all the different places where she has slept, other than her father's farm—the convent, Tostes, the night at La Vaubyessard, and now here. She falls asleep with the thought that her life won't be any worse than it was before, and with the hope that it will be better. In this regard, her conversation with Léon seems like a good omen.

CHAPTER 3

Her first morning in Yonville, Emma wakes up and sees Léon in the town square, on his way to work. She nods to him and quickly closes the window. What does this gesture tell you about her feelings for him?

NOTE: Remember the symbolism of the window. When Emma sees Léon through the open window, it is a sign that she is looking for more than Charles can offer. By shutting the window, Emma closes off her sudden feelings for Léon. She has not yet begun to break through the moral and social pressures working against her—that is, against adultery—but there is no question that her body has begun to give her signs of mounting tension.

Léon's conversation with Emma the night before was apparently an important occasion for him. Never before has he spoken to a woman for such a long time, nor has he been able to express himself so eloquently on such a wide range of subjects.

As the Bovarys settle down in Yonville, Homais proves to be a helpful neighbor. You learn that he's been practicing medicine in the back of his pharmacy without a diploma, and since this is a violation of the law, he's anxious to make friends with the doctor so that Charles will defend him to the authorities if necessary.

Charles isn't particularly happy in his new surroundings. He has few patients and spends most of his time doing odd jobs around the house. He's worried about money, but that doesn't prevent him from taking pleasure in Emma's pregnancy. Emma is disappointed that she doesn't have enough money to buy fancy clothing for the child. She wants a little boy, feeling that males have more opportunities than females in the world. When she gives birth to a girl, she turns away and faints.

NOTE: For Emma, pregnancy and giving birth are interesting as new experiences, but otherwise they seem to have little meaning. There is no place in a life of romance for taking care of a baby, and some readers feel that she senses the child will tie her down even further to a life she despises. For Charles, on the other hand, the birth of the child is the crowning achievement of his life.

Emma decides to name her daughter Berthe, remembering that at the ball she'd heard the Marquis call a woman by that name. As a new mother, Emma enjoys the attention of all the townspeople, but otherwise remains unsatisfied. One day, Emma feels the need to see her daughter, who's living at the house of a wet-nurse, a woman employed to breastfeed another's baby. On the way she meets Léon who accompanies her. By evening, all of Yonville knows that Emma and Léon spent the afternoon together.

NOTE: The people of Yonville feel that Emma, as a married woman, has "compromised herself" by walking with a man who isn't her husband. Emma's values are contrasted with the narrow-mindedness of middle-class small-town people, and her scorn for public opinion foreshadows her future infidelities.

At the wet-nurse's house, Emma picks up her child and begins to sing to her, but the child throws up on the collar of her dress—an act that horrifies Emma. Is Emma's attitude toward her child consistent with what you know of her personality?

As they walk back to town, Emma and Léon talk about a company of Spanish dancers that is coming to perform in Rouen. Their words seem less important, however, than the emotions between them. Emma returns home and Léon, unable to work, climbs to the top of a hill at the edge of the forest and thinks about how different Emma is from all the other people in Yonville. Despite his excitement, the idea of pursuing their intimacy frightens him and offends his middle-class sensibility.

CHAPTER 4

Emma spends the winter dreaming idly at her window. Life in Yonville, it seems, is no more interesting than life in Tostes, and the highlight of her day is a glimpse of Léon as he walks from his office to the inn. In the evenings, Homais visits while the Bovarys are eating dinner. Charles and the pharmacist discuss Charles' patients, and Homais tries to impress them with his knowledge of current events and politics.

Every Sunday, Charles and Emma attend a small gathering at the pharmacist's house. This is the major social event of the week. While Charles and Homais play dominoes, Emma and Léon turn the pages of the latest fashion magazines and recite poems to one another. Though there's an obvious bond between the two, Charles notices nothing improper.

NOTE: Flaubert characterizes Charles as a person "little inclined to jealousy." It's one thing not to be jealous, but another to be blind to what's happening around you. Charles has so little understanding of his wife that he can't imagine she isn't completely happy with their marriage. Consequently, he can't see Léon or any other man as a threat. Blindness and an inability to communicate are two of the major themes of the novel. It might be interesting to take each of the major characters and see in what way they're afflicted with these two conditions.

From her window, Emma can see Léon tending his garden. She makes him a wool bedspread, and everyone in the town concludes that she must be his mistress. What do you think Emma has in mind by giving Léon this gift? Some readers feel that a bedspread is something a mother might give a son, not a gift between lovers. Other readers feel that the gift is Emma's attempt to publicize her feelings for Léon, and by so doing fly in the face of public opinion. Some regard the bedspread as a symbol of Emma's desire to make Léon's bed her own. Léon is confused by her act of generosity and tries to write letters to Emma declaring his love, but always tears them up.

NOTE: Held in by the restraints of her time, as well as by her fears and inexperience, Emma is forced to communicate her emotions for Léon in symbolic words and gestures. Again, the window plays a role in highlighting her need to look beyond the stifling world of Yonville and Bovary. She wants something very deeply—love—but does not know how to attain it. At this point she is still a simple country girl with the *potential* for sophistication, but without the experience to act on her own desires. She is not even sure about them, since her reading has led her to believe that love comes suddenly "with great thunderclaps and flashes of lightning."

CHAPTER 5

One Sunday in February, the Bovarys, Léon, Homais and his children, and Justin, the pharmacist's assistant, take an excursion to see a spinning mill that's being built on the outskirts of Yonville. Homais, as usual, talks at length about how important the mill is going to be but no one's particularly interested. The trip gives Emma a chance to compare Charles and Léon. While her husband is the image of the country bumpkin, Léon has big blue eyes turned toward the clouds—the vision of a young prince.

NOTE: Homais is excited about the new spinning mill because to him it's a symbol of industrial progress. Emma has gone with them for the opportunity of being with Léon. As in the scene at the inn, Flaubert divides the characters into two distinct pairs; Homais and Charles stand for the advancement of middle-class values, while Emma and Léon represent the values of Romanticism. The scene also presents a contrast between ugliness (industrial life) and beauty (romantic love).

Alone in her house the night after this excursion, Emma fantasizes about Léon and remembers the way he looked at her that afternoon. She concludes that he must be in love with her. The next day, she receives the first of many visits from the shady Lheureux, the drygoods merchant who is always stooped in a bent position that evidences his crooked character.

He brags about his contacts with all the leading shopkeepers in Rouen and about his ability to get Emma anything she needs. He shows her his latest wares, and when she decides not to buy anything, he says that money isn't important—that she can pay him any time. He even offers to lend her money if she needs it.

NOTE: This is the beginning of the financial disaster that will ruin Emma and Charles. The credit extended to Emma is a sign of Lheureux's middleclass desire to exploit people for all they are worth. His name, incidentally, means "the Happy One."

When Léon visits that evening, Emma goes out of her way to praise her husband, further confusing the young clerk, who now assumes that she must not like him. Whenever Léon comes to the house, he sees an image of perfect marital bliss, and can't imagine how he ever entertained the idea that Emma might love him. In reality, Emma is frightened by her runaway feelings for Léon. The only way she knows to control them is to deny them.

Though she appears to be the model of virtue, at least in regard to Charles, Emma's real feelings are evident in her physical state. She stops eating and lapses into long silences when she's with other people. Whenever Léon leaves the Bovary house, Emma rushes to the window and watches him walk down the street. Her secret desires for love and money result in a life of anguish.

CHAPTER 6

After daydreaming about her life in the convent, Emma thinks that Father Bournisien might be able to help her, so she heads for the church. But when she arrives, the priest, his cassock covered with grease spots and snuff stains, doesn't recognize her. When he finally remembers her, and she tries to tell him about her unhappiness, he responds by saying that he too is suffering. What do you think he means by this? Though distracted continuously by the boys playing in the church, he advises her to consult her husband about her condition. Finally he excuses himself and runs shouting into the church to see what the boys are doing. If you've ever sought help from a guidance counselor or teacher who was too busy to deal with you or too obtuse to sense that you had a real problem, you may appreciate Emma's feelings at this moment.

For Bournisien, religion is something that's taken for granted, not something you genuinely feel. He's a materialist who thinks the only causes for suffering are lack of food and warmth. Like Charles, he's an example of blindness and is a poor communicator.

Emma returns home and sinks despondently into her armchair. What can she do now? Her daughter Berthe attempts to amuse her, but Emma pushes her away and Berthe falls, cutting her cheek on the edge of the dresser. Guiltily, Emma takes the child upstairs and sits with her until she stops crying. "How ugly that child is," she thinks, as she stares at Berthe's tear-stained face. Does Emma's attitude shock you? Hasn't Flaubert prepared you for the fact that, while Emma dreams of love in the abstract, she has little feeling for real people?

And what is Léon feeling? He has no real ties to anyone in Yonville. He can leave whenever he wants, and if Emma isn't going to return his love, there's no reason for him to stay. Like Emma, he's consumed by fantasies and begins to imagine a life in Paris. Finally he writes to his mother, setting forth his reasons for wanting to move to Paris, then makes plans for his departure. Does it seem odd to you that he should require his mother's permission to take this step? In this respect, is he any different from Charles? Léon seems every bit as conventional as Charles and the other residents of Yonville. His romantic fancies, like Emma's, may just be the result of too many bad books. Watch for the return of Léon at the end of Part Two.

The time comes for Léon to leave Yonville and he goes to see Emma one last time. After kissing Berthe good-bye, he shakes hands awkwardly with Emma and runs down the street to the carriage.

After he leaves, Emma stands by her window and watches the clouds gather in the west. That evening, Homais and Charles speculate on what Léon's life in Paris will be like, while Emma remains silent. As he leaves, Homais informs them of the latest news: the agricultural show will be held in Yonville later this year.

NOTE: Pathetic fallacy   Notice that the weather—gray, cloudy skies—is in harmony with Emma's mood. As Léon leaves, Emma grows even more unhappy. Her tears, like raindrops, are a sign of rough times ahead. The technique of using weather to reinforce a person's emotions is called the *pathetic fallacy*. This is just another way that Flaubert reveals inner states by referring to outside objects.

CHAPTER 7

After Léon leaves, Emma feels as if she's in mourning. She replays in her mind all their joyous moments together—the walks along the river, afternoons in the garden, and so on. She realizes that his company was the only real pleasure in her life, and she curses herself for not seizing this happiness.

NOTE: Indirect narration   The opening paragraphs of Chapter 7 that describe Emma's despair at the loss of Léon are a good example of the indirect narrative that Flaubert uses to reveal a character's thoughts without having the character speak in his or her own voice (first person), and without making the narrator (third-person) appear to be directly commenting. Notice the skill with which he moves back and forth from the narrator to Emma. In a sentence like, "Ah! he was gone, the only charm of her life. . . ." there is no evident narrator and yet Emma is not being quoted. In another sentence, "And she cursed herself for not having loved Léon," Emma's actions are described by the narrator who has taken over. The alternation of narratives is rhythmical and keeps a balance between action and thought. Though some readers complain that there's not enough action in *Madame Bovary*, others feel that the main story of the novel is what's happening inside Emma's head.

The intensity of Emma's love for Léon fades, but her depression and hatred for Charles remain. She tries to console herself by buying expensive clothing from Lheureux and by changing her hairstyle. She even attempts to read history and philosophy—a change from her usual diet of romance novels—but can't concentrate for more than a few pages. Charles, unaware of his wife's unhappiness, takes notice when she begins to spit blood. He writes his mother for advice and asks her to visit them. The elder Madame Bovary suggests that Emma has too much free time on her hands and advises her to go to work. Emma's worst offense, in her mind, is the fact that she spends her time reading novels. Considering the influence that her reading has on her, can you disagree with Charles' mother? Also, see if the theme of honest work as a solution comes up in other contexts. How many of the inhabitants of Yonville could be said to engage in honest work?

After Charles' mother leaves, Monsieur Rodolphe Boulanger de la Huchette, whose name indicates his aristocratic status, arrives at the Bovary household, asking Charles to bleed him since he feels "prickly all over."

NOTE: During the nineteenth century, bleeding was thought to be a general cure for many ailments. As a child, Flaubert probably watched his father perform this procedure on his patients at the hospital in Rouen.

During the bloodletting, Justin, who's holding the basin, faints. When Rodolphe and Charles talk about fainting, Emma tries to impress them by saying that she's never fainted in her life. You know, however, that she fainted after learning that her child was a girl. Why do you think Emma tells this lie? Rodolphe is charmed by Emma and can't understand how a "clumsy oaf" like Charles ever managed to snare such an elegant wife. Rodolphe is thirty-four, a bachelor, and lives on a nearby estate. He's had a great many lovers and is known to be a good judge of women. After meeting her, he can tell how bored she is and imagines how pleasurable it would be to make love to Emma. His only worry, however, is that he won't be able to rid himself of her afterward. He begins to devise a plan to seduce her and concludes that the opening of the agricultural show will provide a good opportunity to see her again.

NOTE: Though Léon never made love to Emma, he plays a crucial role in Emma's transition from marital fidelity to adultery. He helps prepare the way for her first real lover—Rodolphe. Whereas Léon was shy and hesitant, Rodolphe is experienced and dashing, like the brutal, passionate lovers that Emma envisions. He, in his turn, prepares the way for Emma's headlong return to an older and more hardened Léon, the second and last romance of Emma's life.

CHAPTER 8

The agricultural show is a major social occasion in Yonville. Early in the morning, as a crowd begins to gather on the main street, Homais and Madame Lefrançois meet outside the inn, where Homais delivers a lecture on the link between farming and chemistry. While they're talking, they see Emma and Rodolphe walking arm in arm down the street.

NOTE: Do you find it odd that Emma and Rodolphe would make such a public display of their new relationship? Where do you think Charles fits in to this scenario? Does Emma care about Charles' reactions or about those of the townspeople? By bringing the two lovers together so soon after their initial meeting, Flaubert means to underline Rodolphe's seductive powers and Emma's desperate vulnerability.

Rodolphe tells Emma of his sadness and boredom with life in the country. Do you find his words convincing. How does Emma react? Does she know that Rodolphe is playing games with her feelings? He tries to appeal to her sympathy and love for melodrama by saying that so much of life has passed him by, that he's always been alone, and that what he yearns for most is a woman who will give him her undying affection and love. He seems to understand perfectly what Emma is all about.

NOTE: Compare the descriptive passages in this chapter to the description of Charles and Emma's wedding and to that of the ball at La Vaubyessard. Notice especially Flaubert's description of animals, and his use of the same language and tone to describe both people and animals. Remember that Flaubert uses description as a form of commentary on individuals and society. What do you think he's trying to say about human nature in this chapter?

As the main speaker at the fair arrives, you catch a glimpse of Hippolyte, the stable boy at the inn, who will later play an important part in Charles Bovary's life. For the moment, you see him as he takes the horses from the speaker's carriage and leads them to the stable, limping on his clubfoot.

Rodolphe leads Emma to the second floor of the town hall where they can sit comfortably and watch the ceremonies down below. Their position above the action is a commentary on how they stand in relation to the rest of the town. The deputy opens the fair by paying tribute to the present French government and by describing a life where everyone in the country—worker, businessman, and landowner—can go to sleep without fear. Does his speech echo the platitudes of innumerable speeches, spoken by innumerable politicians, down through time? Or is he saying something original?

NOTE: Once again, Flaubert employs the technique of parallel conversations as a counterpoint component of the scene he is orchestrating. If you compare the conversation between Emma and Rodolphe to the speeches of the orators at the fair, you see that both are studded with lies, clichés, and posturing. Both conversations are equally at odds with true feeling and meaningful communication, despite their superficial differences in subject matter. No one in the audience is really listening to the orator, who, like Rodolphe, is merely expressing the thoughts and feelings that he thinks his audience wants to hear. And Emma herself is so blind to her own motivations that she cannot see the lack of genuine feeling behind Rodolphe's words. What's more, Rodolphe does not hear the sincerity and desperate need in Emma's words.

Rodolphe patiently tries to appeal to Emma's romantic nature by telling her that "our duty is to feel what's great and cherish what's beautiful—not to accept the conventions of society and the ignominy it forces on us!" Though Emma argues that it's necessary to heed some of the opinions and values of society, some would say that she doesn't really mean it. Others might point out that Emma has a lot of middle-class characteristics, like her love for material things and her ability to discriminate between the fake and the real. Emma is not quite ready to rise above her own bourgeois upbringing.

As the speeches down below drone on, Rodolphe leans forward and stares intently at Emma. For a moment he reminds her of the Viscount at the ball at La Vaubyessard. She looks into the distance and sees "Hirondelle," the carriage, coming down the road—the same carriage that Léon took when he left town. *Hirondelle* is the French word for a swallow, which suggests that the carriage is a symbol of flight (escape from the mundane). See how this symbol works for other carriage rides that occur in *Madame Bovary*. The smell of Rodolphe's hair—so close to her—intermingles with the smell of the ivy twined around the columns of the town hall. She awakens from her momentary reverie of Léon, and from the thought of the love that escaped her when he left.

The new speaker on the platform is discussing the connection between religion and farming. As he begins to award prizes for the best livestock and crops, Rodolphe takes Emma's hand and thanks her for not drawing away from him.

NOTE: Most readers agree that this is one of the most humorous and ironic moments in the book. As Rodolphe takes Emma's hand and continues plying her with a string of phony endearments, a first prize is awarded for "manures." You might want to reread this chapter and note other instances where Flaubert is making humorous contrasts.

Rodolphe and Emma sit together in silence, their fingers intertwined. After the ceremony, Rodolphe takes Emma home. That night there's a huge feast, with all the residents of Yonville in attendance. Rodolphe sees Emma, but she's with Charles and he makes no attempt to confront her. After the fireworks, the townspeople say good-night and retire to their homes.

NOTE: This is an important chapter because it exemplifies Flaubert's writing at its finest. The humor and irony that weave together the apparently unrelated talk of lovers and petty officials are a masterful way of presenting Emma and Rodolphe's attraction to one another. Notice the purely descriptive passages, the biting manner in which the pompous authorities are portrayed, and the parallels between the animal and human worlds. The peasant woman's faithful service to the farm is contrasted with the fleeting affections that Emma will receive from Rodolphe and her disloyalty to Charles. And the manure that wins first prize in the show is a parallel to the "manure" of Rodolphe's speech to Emma.

Notice that the award given to Catherine Leroux for her long service marks one of the few occasions in the novel where goodness is present, much less rewarded. *Madame Bovary* continues to be criticized by readers who find Flaubert's view of mankind totally negative.

CHAPTER 9

As part of his seduction plan, Rodolphe stays away from Emma for six weeks, reasoning that if she were in love with him before, his long absence will only make her love him more intensely. When he sees her again—alone in the parlor of her house, with the sun going down at the windows (her usual location for reveries)—he knows his calculations were accurate. At first he explains his long absence by saying that he'd been ill. But then he says the thought of her drove him crazy, and that he couldn't bear the idea of her marriage to another man. Finally, he confesses his love for her just as Charles walks in the door.

Rodolphe tells Charles that they were discussing Emma's health and suggests that horseback riding might be good for her. Charles, in his usual undiscriminating, blind way, notices nothing wrong with Rodolphe and Emma's being alone together. He even insists that Emma take up horseback riding, and offers to buy her a new riding outfit.

On a misty day in early October that suitably mirrors the romantic situation Emma longs for, Emma and Rodolphe ride into the forest. After a while they dismount and lead their horses into a clearing where they sit on a log and Rodolphe professes his love for her. At first Emma resists him, but in the end she falls into his arms.

NOTE: The knight in armor Emma idealizes Rodolphe. He represents the romantic knight on horseback, whom she read about in innumerable novels. Some readers feel that Flaubert's decision to place the seduction scene in a natural setting indicates his own mixed feelings about Romanticism. Is he championing Emma for following her feelings in this instance? Other readers feel that Flaubert uses the natural landscape as a means of contrasting the true beauty of nature with Rodolphe's coarseness and manipulations. Knowing

Rodolphe's character, do you feel any sympathy for Emma at this point? Is she a fool? Or has she acted heroically by stepping beyond the boundaries of her middle-class life?

That night, after dinner, Emma shuts herself in her room and relives the events of the afternoon. Staring in the mirror, she sees herself as a changed person. "I have a lover," she murmurs, as if the impossible had finally happened. She thinks of all the heroines she has read about, and now she has been seduced as many of them were.

Emma and Rodolphe spend the next few days riding and making love. Emma confides her unhappiness to him, and they vow to write to one another every day. One morning, filled with a need to see her lover, she visits Rodolphe at La Huchette, his estate. From that point on, this becomes a habit. She waits until Charles leaves for work, then dresses and races across the fields into her lover's arms. One morning, however, when she arrives unexpectedly at La Huchette, Rodolphe's estate, he seems displeased. He tells her that he thinks she's being too reckless and that she's compromising herself by visiting him so frequently. While this may be true, most readers conclude that Rodolphe has grown tired of Emma and reminds her of public opinion in order to ease out of the relationship. Rodolphe is obviously not the gallant knight in shining armor. He is all too human and as flawed as Charles or Léon, and Emma will soon learn that she has been used. Her "perfect" lover is a scoundrel, and their "ideal" romance is but a shoddy affair. Try as she might, Emma cannot succeed as a romantic heroine. The realities of life are too harsh.

CHAPTER 10

Emma is haunted by the idea that someone will find out about her affair with Rodolphe. One morning, returning from her lover's estate, she meets Captain Binet, who's out duck hunting. She lies to him, saying that she's been to the wet-nurse's house to see her baby, even though everyone in Yonville knows that Berthe has been living with her parents for a year.

That same night, Charles, thinking his wife looks unhappy and wanting to distract her, takes Emma to the pharmacist's house after dinner, where she accidentally meets Binet again. The tax-inspector makes a reference to meeting Emma that morning, but luckily for her, Charles doesn't notice anything. The next day Emma and Rodolphe decide that they must act more discreetly. Rodolphe promises to look for a "safe" house in Yonville, but meanwhile the lovers meet in the garden. Emma waits until Charles is asleep, then slips into the darkness, half-dressed. On rainy nights they meet in Charles' consulting room.

Though he's occasionally embarrassed by her extreme sentimentality, Rodolphe is also affected by the passion in Emma's love. Yet the very intensity of her feelings allows him to take her for granted. Emma notices the change in his attitude and begins to regret ever having given in to him. She feels helpless because she realizes how much she's in Rodolphe's power. After six months, they resemble "a married couple placidly keeping a domestic affair alive." Again, reality is encroaching on the dream.

Every year, to commemorate the mending of his broken leg by Charles years ago, Emma's father sends them a turkey. This year, he sends a letter along with the present. Emma is troubled by the way her affair with Rodolphe is going, and the letter makes her think back to her life with her father when she seemed happier. She sees Berthe rolling around playfully on the grass and experiences a sudden burst of love for her daughter.

NOTE: Notice the way Emma's memory plays tricks on her. When she's unhappy in the present, she romanticizes the past. If she can't actually escape her present reality, she can certainly escape it by way of her imagination. The sudden change of attitude toward her child also indicates a longing for innocence and for a way of life that she "should" lead as a mother.

That night she acts coldly toward Rodolphe, but he ignores her. She wonders why she continues the affair, and wants to love Charles but doesn't know what she can do to get close to him.

CHAPTER 11

Homais tells Emma that he's learned about a new method for curing clubfoot. He suggests that Charles learn the medical procedures and perform an operation on Hippolyte, the lame stable boy at the Lion d'Or. Emma is eager to do something to help her husband, and Homais convinces her that Charles' reputation will soar if the operation is successful.

Hippolyte is wary. All the townspeople—interested primarily in the renown such an operation would bring to Yonville—urge him to go through with it. He finally agrees to do so when he realizes that it will cost him nothing, but he feels somehow that it is a mistake. The operation seems a success, and for the first time, Charles has done something to make Emma proud of him. The night after the operation, they sit around talking about their future and the change in their lives once Charles becomes a "famous" doctor. As they prepare for bed, Homais arrives with an article he's written for the local paper, publicizing the "surgical experiment."

NOTE: As you read the description of the operation, remember that Flaubert was the son of a surgeon and that he spent his childhood observing his father at work. Flaubert himself said that growing up in a hospital environment, surrounded by death and suffering, was a major influence on his attitudes about writing, especially about the ideas of objectivity and detachment. He had also been exposed to the malpractice of incompetent doctors and its ruinous results.

Emma's happiness with Charles, however, is shattered five days later. Hippolyte's foot has become a "shapeless mass" and eventually gangrene sets in. Charles attempts to ease the pain but without any success, so he finally calls in another physician, Dr. Cavinet, who announces that Hippolyte's leg will have to be amputated. This old-fashioned doctor—a kind of domineering bully—

criticizes the townspeople, especially Homais, for
thinking that the operation could succeed.

NOTE: Neither Emma nor Homais cares about
what Charles or Hippolyte are feeling. Emma tricks
herself into believing that her husband is capable
of performing such an operation, and after he fails,
she gives up even the pretense of trying to be faithful to him.

Charles is despondent. While Cavinet performs
the amputation, Charles remains at home and tries
to determine what went wrong with the operation.
For Emma, thinking only of herself, it's the final
humiliation. How, she asks herself, could she ever
imagine that someone like Charles might amount
to anything? As Emma and Charles sit like strangers
in front of the fireplace they hear the cries of the
suffering stable boy. In his unhappiness, Charles
begs Emma for a kiss, but she refuses him and
rushes to her room. Later that night, she meets
Rodolphe in the garden and throws herself into
his arms.

NOTE: The operation   In this chapter, Flaubert's
attention to realistic detail enhances your understanding of the amputation. The vocabulary includes words which describe the smell of gangrene, the physical deterioration of Hippolyte's leg,
and the anguish of human suffering. The Romantics would have used lofty, poetic images to dis-
guise the unpleasant details or not described it at
all. The Realists and Naturalists, however, will tell

the truth, regardless of its unpleasantness. Notice that the clubfoot scene delays the progress of the Emma-Rodolphe love affair. It is Flaubert's way of intensifying Emma's disdain for Charles and of strengthening her need for escape. This explains why, at the chapter's end, she flings herself into Rodolphe's arms and sets their relationship back in motion. With each new reason to despise Charles, Emma has one less reason to feel guilt about her affair. Though she is headed for disaster, she believes that happiness—with Rodolphe—lies just around the corner.

CHAPTER 12

Emma complains to Rodolphe about her horrible life and begs him to take her away from Yonville. Rodolphe has never seen his relationship with Emma as anything more than a passing fancy. The last thing he wants is to be attached to her. With each day, Emma's love for Rodolphe increases in proportion to the disgust she feels for Charles. After the failure of the clubfoot operation, she can barely stand to be in the same room with him. Fearing that Rodolphe is growing tired of her, she wears new makeup and jewelry in order to attract him. Her maid, Félicité, spends the day ironing Emma's lingerie, while Justin, who secretly loves Emma, looks on in amazement. From Lheureux she purchases all the latest items from Paris, including an expensive riding crop for Rodolphe. Lheureux doesn't ask for the money immediately, but one day he suddenly shows up with a bill for all her new purchases. Emma doesn't have the money but manages to pay with money from one of Charles' patients. This is the first occasion where her economic and emotional problems become intertwined. As if realizing that things are getting out of hand, Emma promises herself that she's going to economize.

NOTE: This chapter marks the beginning of the end for Emma. She turns away from Charles and puts herself in the hands of Rodolphe and Lheureux, the two most conniving characters in the book. Flaubert's hatred of the middle-class world is evident in his characterization of Lheureux, who not only lusts for power and recognition—as does Homais—but takes pleasure in ruining and humiliating other people. He realizes that Emma is buying presents for her lover and that at some point he'll be able to use this knowledge against her. Compared to people like Rodolphe and Lheureux, Emma seems innocent and unsophisticated.

Emma's gifts, compounded by her overbearing nature, begin to embarrass Rodolphe. The novelty of their relationship has worn off. He has succeeded in making her fall in love with him, and her words of endearment—"I'm your servant and your concubine! You're my king, my idol!"—are the same words he's heard from countless other women. He begins treating her sadistically and coarsely, taking pleasure in seeing just how much she'll do for him. Infatuated with her lover, Emma begins to flaunt public opinion, walking through the streets of Yonville with Rodolphe, smoking cigarettes and staring defiantly at those who seem shocked by her behavior.

Charles' mother visits and one night discovers Félicité with her lover. The parallel between Emma and her maid emphasizes the vulgar nature of Emma's affair, stripped of all its heated romantic trimmings. To seal this identification, Flaubert has Félicité run off with Emma's clothes after her mistress dies.

Once again, Emma pleads with Rodolphe to take her away. She's been suffering for four years—or so she tells her lover—and can no longer bear it. Rodolphe agrees to run away with her, if only to appease his lover at that moment.

The idea that she's finally going to escape from her life in Yonville alters Emma's attitude toward Charles. But she is only going through the motions. What's the point of being angry at someone you'll never see again? All her thoughts are focused on the day of escape. The transformation is physical as well. Never before has she looked so beautiful, and Charles, who is completely ignorant of his wife's plans, becomes infatuated with her again.

While lying awake in bed, Emma dreams of herself and Rodolphe on horseback, gliding over the mountains. She plays out the various scenarios of the future in her head while Charles snores beside her and Berthe, whom she plans to take along with her, coughs in her sleep.

NOTE: The idea of "flight" is another characteristic of the romantic nature. Remember that Emma always thinks that change for its own sake is a way of improving things. What is the difference between change for its own sake and change calculated to improve one's lot?

With the trip only a month away, Emma orders a long cloak, a trunk, and an overnight bag from Lheureux. A few days before the date of departure, Rodolphe arrives in the garden and Emma thinks that he looks sad.

NOTE: Emma's need for Rodolphe   What do you think is going on in Rodolphe's mind? On the basis of what you know about him it must be clear that he has no intention of running off with Emma, but at this moment he's unable to tell her the truth. Some readers feel that Emma knows that Rodolphe has no intention of escaping with her and that she's made herself vulnerable to him because she wants to suffer. Others believe in her inability to see into Rodolphe's true nature. Still others feel that Emma wouldn't be happy even if Rodolphe *did* run away with her. Yet as she clings to him in the garden and tells him that she'll do anything for him, there's no doubt that at this moment her love for him is genuine.

After the lovers part, Rodolphe stops and looks back. He sees Emma in her white dress, disappearing into the shadows. He leans against a tree, moved by the intensity of her love for him, and realizes that he'd be a fool to go off with her. "Just the same, though," he says to himself, "she was a pretty mistress."

CHAPTER 13

Rodolphe returns home and composes a letter to Emma. Before doing so, he takes out all her old souvenirs and rereads her letters. While he's going through this array of objects and letters, he finds mementos from other mistresses and is amused to think of all the women who have loved him.

Do you have the feeling he's written similar letters to other women? Writing this type of "Goodbye" letter is for him an inevitable part of the game between men and women. He tells Emma that at some point they would have grown tired of each other and that she would have felt remorse for having left her husband. "Forget me," he advises, "only fate is to blame."

NOTE: Flaubert employs the notion of fate several times in the book. Later on, Charles finds the letter to Emma, and after her death, when he meets Rodolphe face to face, he repeats this very statement about fate back to him. In these two instances, it's the simplest way of explaining things. Do you think that Emma's downfall is inevitable given her basic nature? Is Flaubert suggesting that people cannot change or only Emma?

Rodolphe continues his letter and ends by saying that he's going to leave the country to avoid the temptation of seeing her again. He lets a drop of water spill on the page to blot the ink and give the impression of tears. Then, satisfied that he's done his job properly, he smokes his pipe and goes to bed.

The next day, Emma receives the letter and reads

it at the window looking out over the town. For a moment, as her heart races, she thinks of leaping to the pavement below, but her thoughts of suicide are interrupted by Charles' voice, calling her to come eat.

As Emma contemplates suicide, she hears the droning sound of Binet's lathe, symbolizing the boredom and emptiness of the life she now faces. Flaubert makes skillful use of this motif.

At dinner, Charles mentions that he heard news that Rodolphe was taking a trip. At the sound of her lover's name, Emma begins choking. Suddenly, the carriage carrying Rodolphe out of town passes the house, and Emma—recognizing him in the glow of the lantern—cries out and collapses. Homais brings some vinegar from the pharmacy in an attempt to revive her but she faints again. "The letter! Where is it?!" she shrieks, thinking that her husband is going to find Rodolphe's message. But both Charles and Homais think she's delirious, and in fact they're right. Her illness following Rodolphe's departure was set up earlier by her illness following the ball at La Vaubyessard. Each expectation of new heights brings Emma crashing down to reality as her expectations are crushed. Be prepared for a similar crash to reality in Part Three.

Charles abandons his practice to stay at his wife's bedside. Does his devotion to Emma at this point make him seem more sympathetic in your eyes? Her illness lasts forty-three days, during which she neither speaks nor eats. Finally, she has enough strength to leave her bed and take a walk in the garden, but when she sees the bench where she and Rodolphe made love, she collapses once again. This second phase of her illness is even more complicated than the first, and her fits of nausea make Charles wonder whether she has cancer. On top of all this, he now has financial troubles as well.

NOTE: Suicide From this point on, Emma will think about suicide as the only certain escape from the miseries of life. The idea of suicide as an alternative to a failed love affair is another typical convention of some Romantic literature, which had been inspired by an early work of the German writer, Johann Wolfgang von Goethe, *The Sorrows of Young Werther*. In this work, and its many imitations, suicide is considered preferable to life without the ideal love. The introduction of suicide as a way out also foreshadows Emma's final escape.

CHAPTER 14

Charles' financial problems are enumerated here in great detail. Not only does he owe Homais for all the medicine supplied during Emma's illness, but Lheureux, the merchant, is after him to pay for all of Emma's purchases. Charles unwisely decides to borrow money at a high interest rate from Lheureux himself, hoping that after a year he'll be able to catch up with his bills.

Emma's illness lingers through the winter. She sits by her familiar window while the monotonous rhythms of town life hum around her. Occasionally, Father Bournisien visits her. At the height of her illness she had asked for Communion and had experienced a celestial vision where she imagined herself ascending to heaven. As she recovers, the memory of the vision gives her hope that there's a "bliss greater than worldly happiness, a different kind of love transcending all others."

NOTE: Here is another occasion when Flaubert links Emma's religious and sexual feelings, just as he did when describing her life at the convent school. Do you think that her devotion to God is any different from her feelings for Rodolphe?

During her recovery, she becomes a more attentive parent and takes a renewed interest in the household. She receives daily visits from most of the women in the town and from Justin, who has a secret crush on her. Homais suggests that going to the opera in Rouen might amuse Emma. At first, Emma refuses, but Charles insists and eventually they decide to go.

NOTE: As Emma and Charles changed location between Parts One and Two, so too the focus of Part Three will change to the large Normandy city of Rouen. This provides another chance for Emma's hopes to be realized. A city like Rouen represents to her a chance for exciting adventure. (The city of her ultimate fantasy, Paris, will never be achieved.) You already probably know enough about Emma to realize that a change is only a temporary cure. Do you and your friends ever equate change of place with change of heart?

CHAPTER 15

Emma and Charles arrive at the opera house early. Emma is excited after having been cooped up in Yonville for so long and insists that they stroll along the waterfront before the show. Once inside, she gets caught up in the throng of opera-goers swirling around her. When the opera begins, she immerses herself totally in the romantic story and the soaring music. Charles, understandably, is confused by the story and keeps asking Emma what's going on. She impatiently tells him to keep quiet, as she identifies with the passions of the characters, comparing the hero to Rodolphe. By intermission, Emma is concocting new fantasies about what her life might have been like had she met someone like the tenor who plays the hero. As he takes his bows, she imagines that he's staring directly at her. She feels the impulse to rush into his arms and beg him to carry her away.

NOTE: The opera that Charles and Emma are watching is *Lucia di Lammermoor* by the Italian composer Gaetano Donizetti (1797–1848). It is based on a novel by the Scottish Romantic writer Sir Walter Scott. The tragic love story that ends in madness and suicide would appeal to Emma. Both the story and Emma's new fantasies are omens that are about to take on significance with the reappearance of Léon.

After the intermission, Charles tells Emma that he's just seen Léon. A moment later, the former law clerk from Yonville shows up in their box. Seeing her ex-suitor again makes it hard for Emma to concentrate on the second half of the opera, and they leave before it ends.

NOTE: Emma uses the opera in the same way she used religion—to feed her romantic impulses and to escape from her present situation. In order to bring you closer to Emma's feelings, Flaubert uses the technique of double action, counterpointing Emma's thoughts while watching the opera with the action on stage. Do you recall the other instances where Flaubert has used this technique?

The three of them go to a waterfront café where they discuss Emma's recent illness. Léon, who's been living in Paris, announces that he has returned to Rouen to work for a large law firm, and Charles suggests that Emma remain in Rouen for a few more nights, thinking that she might like to see the opera through to the end. It's hard not to be amazed by Charles' naïveté, but the world of passion and intense emotion is so foreign to him that he just doesn't notice these feelings in other people. When they part for the night, Charles invites Léon to dinner. The clerk, whose feelings about Emma are obvious to everyone but Charles, agrees to come.

As Part Two closes, you might review its high points: its framework of the young Léon at the beginning and the older Léon at the end; the focal event of the agricultural show as backdrop for the seduction of Emma; the two contrasting important events of the bungled operation and the opera; the nasty reality and the romantic dreams that both provoke Emma to attempt escape; and in the background, the mounting debts to Lheureux.

PART III
CHAPTER 1

What has Léon been doing for the last three years? Though he's still a shy person, his experience with the loose women of Paris has given him more confidence. (Remember the way the noblemen at La Vaubyessard in Part One were said to have a practiced hand at controlling horses *and* loose women.) In this regard, he seems like a miniature version of Rodolphe. His first thought, after seeing Emma again, is that he's going to do everything in his power to seduce her.

The day after the opera, Léon goes to the inn where the Bovarys are staying and learns that Charles has returned to Yonville. Emma tries to impress upon Léon that she's become philosophical since they last saw each other. She goes on at length about "the wretchedness of earthly affections and the isolation in which the heart must remain forever," but makes no mention of Rodolphe, the cause of her illness. Léon tells her how bored he's been, how he'd thought of her often when he was in Paris, and how he'd even written her letters that he never mailed.

NOTE Compare the conversation between Léon and Emma with the one between Rodolphe and Emma at the agricultural show. Has Emma learned to judge the sincerity of her suitors? Do you know someone like Emma who is anxious to believe everything people say?

Léon talks of how he sometimes wishes he were dead and that one night he wrote out a will, asking to be buried in the bedspread that Emma had made for him. Like Rodolphe, Léon is taking advantage of Emma's weaknesses—her unhappiness, frustration, and longing for love. Though Léon is more of a romantic than Rodolphe—and in this respect more evenly matched with Emma—his main purpose is still to make a conquest.

As night falls, they sit in Emma's hotel room, reminiscing about the past. Léon attempts to embrace her but she withdraws. Léon insists that they see one another again before she leaves Rouen and suggests that they meet at eleven the next morning in the Cathedral. After he leaves, Emma composes a letter to him, canceling their appointment, but realizes that she doesn't know his address. She decides that she'll give him the letter in person.

NOTE: Once again, Emma is involved wholeheartedly in the drama and intrigue of a love affair. Writing secret letters in an attempt to deny her feelings and then changing her mind at the last minute—excites her. Some readers feel that Emma's problems do not stem from Charles, but rather from the life without turmoil that he represents. For Emma, the only way she can be fully alive is to be in a state of inner conflict.

The next morning, Léon arrives at the church. When Emma sees him, she thrusts the letter into his hand and tells him to read it—but at the same moment, she withdraws the letter and rushes into the chapel to pray. Finally Léon takes Emma's arm and hurries her outside.

NOTE: Flaubert's use of description When writing *Madame Bovary*, Flaubert attempted to describe objects as reflections of the way his characters felt. The description of the Cathedral as a "gigantic boudoir" reflects Emma's attitudes toward religion. You may recall other instances in the book where Flaubert links religion and sexuality. The description of the frenzied cab ride through Rouen that follows the couple's departure from the Cathedral reveals their uncontrolled love-making without once peeking inside the cab, which was "sealed tighter than a tomb and tossing like a ship." In most novels, you learn something about the characters from what they say, but in *Madame Bovary* there is comparatively little dialogue, thanks to Flaubert's indirect style. Some think that the key to the book—and to the hearts and minds of the characters—lies in the descriptive passages.

Léon calls a cab. He stifles Emma's protests by saying that there's nothing improper about what they're doing. Everyone in Paris does it all the time. Léon tells the driver to keep moving, and the cab sets out on a tour of Rouen, blinds drawn. In the middle of the day, as the carriage passes through the countryside, Emma's hand reaches out of the window and she tosses the pieces of her letter to Léon (which look like "white butterflies") into the wind. Do you remember the "black butterflies" of charred paper flower petals that floated from Emma's burning wedding bouquet? What do you think is the connection between the two images? What relation do they have to Emma's marriage?

When the cab finally stops, a woman with a black veil walks away from it without looking back. What do you suppose Emma is feeling at this moment? Has she sealed her fate like the "sealed" cab?

CHAPTER 2

When Emma returns to Yonville, she receives an urgent message instructing her to go to the pharmacy. When she arrives, she finds Homais angrily scolding Justin. Apparently, in the course of making jam, the young man took a pan from Homais' private laboratory. This laboratory is off limits to everyone but the pharmacist. Homais is especially angry because he had kept the pan on the same shelf as a bottle of arsenic. Homais claims that if arsenic had touched the pan, they might all have been poisoned. In his anger, Homais hardly notices Emma, who finally asks Madame Homais why she'd been summoned.

NOTE: This scene is important, as it foreshadows Emma's suicide by means of arsenic poisoning.

The pharmacist reveals that something terrible has happened while Emma was in Rouen: Charles' father has died. She returns home, but even the death of her father-in-law can't distract her from memories of the day spent with Léon. Her only thought is to get away from her husband, whom she finds utterly weak and contemptible.

The next day, Charles' mother arrives in Yonville. Even she is able to pardon her husband for his past offenses, but Emma has no feeling for her late father-in-law. She just wants to be left alone so she can think about Léon.

Lheureux visits and asks to speak with Emma in private. He congratulates her about her forthcoming inheritance and tries to convince Emma that she should begin handling her husband's affairs. This makes sense to Emma, as Charles seems too upset about his father's death to think about practical matters. Lheureux tells Emma that if she had a power of attorney (to act legally for Charles), she could deal directly with him instead of getting Charles' approval.

During the next few days, Emma impresses Charles with her practical knowledge of their financial affairs. Charles suggests that Léon handle their affairs, and Emma agrees to go to Rouen to consult with him. It's a perfect excuse to see her lover again, and she stays in Rouen for three days.

NOTE: In this chapter, Emma's dealings with Lheureux take on a new meaning. Some readers feel that Flaubert is attempting to balance Emma's heartlessness toward Charles by placing her in the role of Lheureux's victim. Others feel that Charles begins to emerge here as the only major character with no desire to hurt anyone else. Compared to Emma, Lheureux, and Léon—who think only of themselves—Charles stands out as a model of compassion, even though he is a plodding dullard.

CHAPTERS 3 and 4

For Emma and Léon, the three days in Rouen are like "a real honeymoon." They stay in an expensive hotel room, behind closed shutters (like a tomb), sipping iced fruit drinks in the morning. In the evening, they hire a boat that takes them to an island to have dinner, and the boatman tells about a lively party of people whom he'd taken to the islands a few days before. One of the party, "a tall, handsome man, named Adolphe or Dodolphe" kept everyone amused. Emma, certain that he's referring to Rodolphe, shudders at the thought of her former lover.

When they part, Emma instructs Léon to write her. He assures her that the legal matters will be taken care of, but that he can't understand why she's so anxious to obtain a power of attorney.

One day, longing to see Emma, Léon leaves his office and travels to Yonville. Emma isn't home, but the next night, in the middle of a thunderstorm, they meet in the garden. Emma promises Léon that she'll devise a plan that will enable them to see each other more frequently. Meanwhile, her relationship with Lheureux has become more complicated. She continues to spend freely, assuming that the inheritance from Charles' father will cover her bills. During the winter, she pretends to develop an intererst in music, and since Charles encourages her, she suggests that she take piano lessons. This means taking private lessons each week in Rouen, and Charles agrees to the plan.

NOTE: As Emma plunges deeper into her affair
with Léon, she also incurs greater debts in order
to support this life-style. Ironically, her love affair
requires money, not just dreams, to support it.
Otherwise, Emma would be unable to make the
trips to Rouen. But she and Charles have no money
and will soon be bankrupt. This financial condition
is merely a reinforcement of Emma's "bankrupt"
love affair with Léon. It also reminds you of Emma's participation in the bourgeois world that she
pretends to despise.

CHAPTER 5

Every Thursday morning Emma makes the trip
from Yonville to Rouen. After she has been clois-
tered in a small town all week, her arrival in the
big city fills her with excitement. She meets Léon
in a hotel room and they embrace passionately,
telling each other how miserable they've been all
week. Do Emma's feelings, at this point, seem
genuine? Does her private world with Léon make
her happy? Is her affair with Léon what she's been
looking for all this time?

NOTE: Emma and Léon's affair differs in many
regards from Emma's affair with Rodolphe. With
Léon, Emma seems to be playing the dominant
role, or teacher, whereas with Rodolphe the roles
were reversed. Emma introduces Léon to the
pleasures of sensuality, just as Rodolphe had done
with her. Some readers feel that Emma is teaching
Léon everything she learned from Rodolphe. In

what other ways are the two relationships different? In what ways are they similar?

Some nights, on her return trip to Yonville, Emma sees a blind old beggar roaming the countryside. As the carriage passes, she can hear his song: "The heat of the sun on a summer day/Warms a young girl in an amorous way." Why does this song affect Emma so intensely? Sometimes the beggar grabs on to the side of the cab and when the coachman realizes this, he strikes the beggar with his whip until the helpless old man falls into the mud at the side of the road.

NOTE: The blind beggar symbolizes the depth of misery to which a person can sink. The sound of his voice "descended into the depths of her soul." Is it possible that Emma sees in the beggar a reflection of herself? Emma will soon be a beggar herself. Having run up enormous debts with Lheureux, she will be forced to beg for money to repay these debts. Flaubert uses the blind old beggar to foreshadow Emma's upcoming disaster. He is also a symbol of the moral and intellectual blindness of the main characters to their own natures and to others' needs.

The days between visits to Léon grow more and more intolerable. One night, Charles informs Emma that Mademoiselle Lempereur—the piano teacher—says that she has never heard of Emma. Emma tries to conceal her deception by saying that the teacher probably forgot her name. It's an unlikely story, but Charles is ready to believe anything. Emma pretends to search frantically for the non-existent receipts, and a few days later Charles "finds" the receipts—obviously forged by Emma—in one of his boots.

One day, leaving the hotel in Rouen with Léon, she meets Lheureux. The greedy merchant realizes that, if necessary, he can blackmail Emma by telling Charles about her affair with Léon. He uses this knowledge to get more money out of her. In a complicated transaction, he convinces her to give him a piece of property that her father-in-law had owned. He has her sign four new promissory notes [written promises to pay a specified sum of money at a stated time] and tells her that she can keep the money from the sale of the house. With this money she pays most of her old debts. The fourth note arrives when Charles—who knows nothing about any of these financial arrangements—is at home. She sits on his lap, caresses him, and tries to explain how the money was spent. Charles, not knowing what to think, writes his mother for advice. The old woman arrives and immediately begins to complain about Emma's extravagant tastes. An argument ensues between the two women, and for the first time in his life, Charles takes his wife's side. His mother, enraged, leaves, threatening never to return to her son's house.

Her triumphs at home make Emma even more reckless in her behavior. She no longer fears compromising herself and walks openly with Léon through the streets of Rouen. One night, when Emma decides not to return to Yonville, Charles takes a carriage to Rouen in the middle of the night and searches for her. They meet accidentally on a street near the piano teacher's house, and Emma lies to him again, saying that she'd been feeling ill and that Charles shouldn't worry every time she stays out late. Charles blindly accepts her explanation, and after this incident, Emma begins going to Rouen whenever she pleases.

NOTE: Emma's life is rapidly disintegrating. Any control she had prior to her Rouen visits is now dwindling to nothing as her financial problems multiply and her marriage falls apart. Any vestiges of respect for the marital structure are now gone. She parades openly with Léon, maintains a hectic extramarital affair, and lies guiltlessly to her husband when questioned about her actions. The rollercoaster ride has begun, and it's only a matter of time before Emma completely destroys herself.

CHAPTER 6

Homais visits Rouen one Thursday—the day Léon and Emma usually meet—and takes Léon to a fancy restaurant, forcing him to miss his appointment with Emma. For the pharmacist, this trip to Rouen is one of his rare chances to escape from Yonville, and he keeps suggesting new things to do. Finally, Léon manages to get away from him and rushes to the hotel to see Emma. But she has departed, furious at him for missing their appointment. After this, Emma's passion for Léon cools down, then flares up again. Even Léon notices her irrational behavior, and wonders where all this madness will lead. He senses trouble ahead, but he can't bring himself to break off with her.

NOTE: As the affair progresses, Léon's middle-class values begin to reassert themselves. Emma is more than he can handle, so he retreats into his bourgeois security. He's about to be promoted to head law clerk in his office and begins to wonder whether his affair with Emma will jeopardize his career. His inability to leave Homais—who represents the middle class—and go to Emma, who represents his romantic side, indicates the direction in which he is headed.

Emma's affair with Léon never completely satisfies her. She still imagines the possibility of a perfect lover, this "strong, handsome man with a valorous, passionate and refined nature, a poet's soul in the form of an angel . . ." At this point, she thinks about nothing but her passions and, as a result, her financial dealings with Lheureux get completely out of hand. A bill, which Lheureux had given to a banker in Rouen, arrives at the house, and the following day a protest of nonpayment is delivered. Lheureux explains that he wants all the money the Bovarys owe him at once. If not, there will be a court judgment and the Bovarys' possessions will be seized. Emma begs for a loan, and Lheureux agrees only when she tells him that she still has some property coming to her from her father-in-law's estate.

In an attempt to raise money, Emma bills all of Charles' patients and begins selling old clothing and household articles. But her finances are so complicated that every time she pays back part of her debt to Lheureux, she has to borrow more money from him. In her confusion about money matters, Emma neglects to take care of her household, spending nights reading romance novels and thinking about her affair with Léon.

Charles is worried about his wife's health—he believes her old illness will recur—but he's too timid to complain, even when she's insulting him.

One evening, after staying up all night at a masked ball in Rouen, Emma returns home to find that a legal document has been issued ordering her to pay all her debts within twenty-four hours. If she doesn't, all her possessions will be confiscated. She rushes to see Lheureux, who not only refuses to help but threatens to tell Charles what he knows about her affair with Léon if she doesn't pay up. He has no more use for her now that she is destitute. When she bursts into tears and tells him that he's destroying her last hope, he acts as if her problems are none of his business and slams the door in her face.

NOTE: As her financial and emotional life falls apart, Emma withdraws more and more into her fantasy world. It's as if she's on a fast-moving train headed nowhere and can't get off. All she can do is indulge her fantasies to even greater excesses. The masked ball symbolizes how far removed she is from reality. She has no ability to deal with her problems and no one to turn to for guidance. All she wants to do is "fly away like a bird and make herself young again somewhere in the vast purity of space."

CHAPTER 7

The next day, the bailiff (a local officer of the court) arrives at the house to make an inventory of Emma and Charles' possessions, though Charles knows nothing about what's going on. Emma travels to Rouen to visit all the bankers who might lend her money, but they all refuse. She asks Léon for help but all he can do is promise to talk to a rich friend and hope that his friend will lend him the money.

Emma returns to Yonville in the same carriage as Homais. They pass the blind man singing at the bottom of the hill. When Homais tosses the man a coin, the beggar squats on his haunches, in thanks, like a starving dog, and Emma tosses him her last coin.

NOTE: You see Emma slowly sinking to the same level as the beggar. Like him, she must go around asking people for money. Tossing him her last coin is a symbolic attempt to place herself on a higher level and to retain some sense of her own dignity and worth—but it's also a sign that she is giving up her worldly possessions in preparation for death.

The next morning Emma awakes to the voices of a crowd in the town square. A notice advertising a public auction has been posted, and Justin is trying to tear it down. Emma, seeing that all her property is for sale, goes to the house of the notary, Monsieur Guillaumin, to arouse his sympathy. He asks her why she never came to him before for help, then drops to his knees and begins to kiss her hand. She leaps to her feet, indignant, and demands the

money. But when all he can say is "I love you,"
she rushes out of his house. Is it finally dawning
on Emma that she is just one step removed from
prostitution?

She goes to Binet and appeals to him as well.
Notice that Flaubert describes this scene indirectly,
through the eyes of the mayor's wife and a friend
who watch Emma and Binet from a distance. Emma
seems to be making a proposition to Binet; whether
it's erotic or not you don't know. Suddenly Binet
cries out: "Madame! You can't be serious!" The
two old women turn and see Emma race down the
street.

Needing time to think things over, Emma goes
to the home of the wet-nurse Madame Rollet. She
remembers Léon's promise and sends Madame
Rollet to her house to see if he's arrived with the
money. Not surprisingly, there's no sign of Léon.
As a last resort, Emma thinks of seeking help from
Rodolphe. She's certain that if she reminds him of
their past love for one another, he'll come to her
rescue. What's your prediction of her success?

CHAPTER 8

As she approaches Rodolphe's estate, Emma
wonders what she'll say when she sees her former
lover. The familiar landscape brings back memories of their affair, but how different things are
now! Is it possible that Rodolphe will have changed
as well?

When she first sees him, he's seated in front of
the fire, smoking his pipe. He leaps up, obviously
surprised to see her, and they discuss the past while
Emma weeps. Rodolphe kneels at her feet and says
he still loves her, but when she asks for 3,000 francs,

he backs away and explains that he doesn't have it.

Rodolphe's rejection is the crushing blow. His home is filled with expensive objects—many of which she gave him—that could be converted into cash. She tries to make Rodolphe feel guilty, but all he says in response to her tirade is that he doesn't have the money. With this, Emma returns to Yonville in a daze.

NOTE: Léon and Rodolphe's unwillingness to help Emma gives her some insight into their selfishness. She feels betrayed, especially by Rodolphe, and this gives her the impetus to kill herself. As she leaves Rodolphe's house, however, she's not thinking about money. "She was now," Flaubert tells you, "suffering only through her love." On the basis of what you know about Rodolphe, do you find his reaction surprising? Emma can't understand how she could love others so much and receive so little in return. Some readers feel that circumstances beyond her control have brought her to the brink of suicide. Others argue that she is solely responsible for her circumstances and refuses to admit her part in creating them.

Back in Yonville, Emma stops in front of the pharmacy, sees Justin, and orders him to give her the key to the upstairs laboratory where Homais keeps his special supply of chemicals. Because Justin is secretly in love with Emma, he can't refuse her. She climbs the steps to the laboratory, finds the bottle of arsenic, and before Justin can do anything, she swallows the poison. Justin, looking on,

becomes frantic, but Emma warns him not to tell
anyone what she's doing. She returns home, "feeling what was almost the serenity of a duty well
done."

NOTE: The young Justin's love for Emma parallels Flaubert's infatuation with the older Elisa
Schlésinger (see the Author and His Times section). In his pure and truly felt love, perhaps Justin, more than anyone, coincides with Emma's image of the ideal lover. Flaubert ironically has Justin
show Emma where the arsenic is located, and then
has him watch as she swallows it. The boy with
the most to offer, stands by helplessly.

Charles has learned that his property is going to
be auctioned. He has searched everywhere for
Emma, and on returning to the house finds her in
the bedroom, writing a letter that she instructs him
not to read until the next day. The arsenic has not
yet taken effect and Emma feels only a bitter taste
in her mouth. As she drinks a glass of water and
suddenly begins choking, Charles notices a white
substance on the side of the basin and begs her to
tell him what she's eaten. When she refuses, he
rushes to her writing desk, reads the letter, and
realizes that Emma has poisoned herself.

Grief-stricken, Charles summons Doctors Canivet and Larivière. Kneeling at the foot of her bed,
he asks, "Weren't you happy? Is it may fault? I did
everything I could!" Emma passes her hand through
Charles' hair and reassures him that nothing was
his fault. What is your reaction to this gesture of
tenderness on Emma's part? Does she have gen-

uine fondness—or even love—for Charles? Or does she finally recognize her own responsibility?

Emma asks to see Berthe one last time. After the little girl is brought to her and then taken away, Emma's suffering becomes more intense and she begins vomiting blood. Canivet and Larivière arrive, but nothing can save her. As Father Bournisien administers the last rites, the blind beggar appears at the window, singing his song: "The wind was blowing hard that day/And Nanette's petticoat flew away." Emma begins laughing horribly, and as her body trembles one last time, she dies.

NOTE: The deathbed scene   Emma's death—an ugly, painful ordeal—concludes the long train of events that have progressively worn her down. Instead of dying the sensual, beautiful death of the romantic heroine, Emma shakes violently while the beggar, a symbol of death, lurks at her window. Notice this final use of the window to express the state of Emma's soul. When she was searching for love, the window was open; when she was making love inside a room, the window was closed. On her deathbed, Emma can see through the window to a world beyond—to the death represented by the old beggar, the final escape.

Notice the parallel between the bungled clubfoot operation and Emma's messy suicide. Both are filled with the most graphic medical details and serve as reminders of the ugly facts of life and death, facts that Emma never could face.

Even as she is on the verge of death, she recalls her first religious (sexual) experiences and summons all her waning strength to kiss passionately the figure of Christ on the crucifix as she receives the last rites. She seems content, as though there is still time for another dream of love. The beggar reminds her of terrifying reality one last time before she dies. Blind to the end, Emma never stops dreaming.

CHAPTERS 9 and 10

Charles weeps over the body of his wife until Homais and Canivet convince him to leave her room. Homais disguises the fact of Emma's suicide by telling everyone that she'd mistaken the arsenic for sugar. What reasons do you think he has for concealing the truth? Homais and Father Bournisien tell Charles to make preparations for Emma's funeral. "Bury her in her wedding gown," he instructs them, "with white shoes and a wreath." Homais and the priest are amazed by Charles' tender feelings, but Charles is burying Emma as he imagines she would want to be. Do you think Emma would want to be buried in her wedding gown?

Charles' mother arrives and complains about the cost of the funeral. Charles flies into a rage in much the same way Emma might have done under similar circumstances. Notice, in fact, how Charles begins to take on Emma's characteristics after her death. Seated beside her body, he daydreams about their past together, remembering the sound of her voice, her gestures and poses. He even performs the romantic act of clipping a lock of her hair.

The people of Yonville pass through the house to see Emma's body and pay their respects to Charles. How do you think they react to Emma's death? Emma's father arrives, but he doesn't know whether his daughter is dead or alive. When Homais wrote him, he phrased the letter so that it was impossible to know what was wrong with her. Why do you think he did this? When Monsieur Rouault learns what happened, he falls into Charles' arms while Homais, with his typically insensitive way, advises them to be philosophical and to act dignified.

NOTE: After Emma dies, Charles tries to keep the spark of romantic feeling alive by "becoming" Emma. Is Flaubert using Emma's death to signal symbolically the death of Romanticism and the emerging power of middle-class life? Homais, with his hypocritical values, and Lheureux represent the future. Do you think Flaubert's vision is overly pessimistic?

At the gravesite, Charles cries out "Good-bye" and tries to throw himself into the grave beside her. Homais, filled with his typical sense of self-importance, regrets that he didn't have time to compose a speech.

Charles and his mother sit up most of the night talking about the future. She offers to live with him in Yonville, secretly pleased that she no longer has a rival for her son's affections, but Charles knows that this would never work. Everyone else in Yonville is asleep. Rodolphe is sleeping peacefully in his château. Léon is asleep in Rouen. The only person still awake is Justin, who's kneeling on Emma's grave, unable to believe that she's dead.

CHAPTER 11

Shortly after Emma's death, Lheureux shows up asking for money. Charles refuses to sell any of his wife's clothing and writes letters to his patients asking them for money, but he doesn't realize that they've already paid Emma. Félicité, Emma's maid, begins to dress in Emma's clothing, and Charles often mistakes her for his wife. Then the word arrives that Léon is getting married.

Going through Emma's things, Charles discovers the letter from Rodolphe, breaking off their affair. Blinded by his grief, Charles refuses to believe that Emma and Rodolphe had ever been lovers. He buys patent-leather boots and begins using perfumed mustache-wax, thinking that this would please his dead wife. If only he had acted this way when she was alive! Gradually he sells the furniture and empties all the rooms in the house except for Emma's bedroom, where he spends days playing with Berthe and repairing her toys. No one visits them. Justin has gone to work at a grocery in Rouen. The blind beggar, who had arrived in Yonville to try a cure prescribed by Homais, spreads the word that the pharmacist is a quack. Homais puts a notice in the newspaper complaining about the blind beggar, and has him committed for life to an asylum.

Looking through Emma's rosewood desk, Charles finally stumbles upon the letters from Léon and Rodolphe. Now there can be no doubt in his mind that Emma was having affairs with them. The discovery leaves him despondent, so he shuts himself up in his house, and people in town gossip that he's drinking heavily.

At the market, where Charles has gone to sell

his horse, he meets Rodolphe. They go for a drink together and Charles, staring at the face of the man who'd been his wife's lover, realizes that he "would like to be that man." What do you think he means by this? How would you have reacted in a similar situation? Rodolphe attempts to steer the conversation to trivial subjects but notices that Charles is becoming more and more agitated. For a moment, it seems that Charles will finally vent his rage, but all he tells Rodolphe is that he doesn't hold what Rodolphe did against him. "Only fate is to blame," he tells Rodolphe, who considers him a weakling for being so passive.

NOTE: Reread Rodolphe's letter to Emma (Part Two, Chapter 13) where he writes "Only fate is to blame"—the exact words Charles uses when he and Rodolphe confront one another—and recall that Charles has just read Rodolphe's letter. Some readers feel that repeating the phrase to his rival is a sign of Charles' dullness and lack of cleverness. Yet others conclude that Charles sincerely feels that fate is the reason for Emma's tragic death. Other readers believe that fate is just an excuse to avoid the truth, and that Charles, to the very end, refuses to blame Emma for their ruin.

The day after meeting Rodolphe, Charles sits broken-hearted on the bench in the garden where Emma and her lovers used to meet. In the evening, when Berthe comes to look for him, she finds him with his eyes closed and a lock of black hair in his hands. She thinks that he's playing, but when she prods him, he falls to the ground, dead. His death, ironically, is right out of a Romantic novel and no doubt would have pleased Emma. Could it be that the only character in *Madame Bovary* who really knows what true love is and, in fact, has died for love, is Charles? In going back over the novel, are there any other indications that Charles has been misrepresented by Emma and Flaubert?

Berthe is sent to live with an aunt, who puts her to work in a cotton mill. Three different doctors, Flaubert tells you, attempt to practice in Yonville, but Homais—who has finally been awarded the decoration of the national Legion of Honor—manages to alienate them all.

NOTE: The conclusion   Flaubert brings everything to a conclusion with the death of Emma. Charles discovers the truth of his wife's affairs with Rodolphe and Léon; the Bovary possessions are sold to pay off debts; Charles and his mother have a final falling-out; Berthe is victimized by the loss of her mother, and almost immediately, the death of her father. Even Homais manages to put his final stamp of authority on the town of Yonville. The novel does not end on an optimistic note. It is a bleak finale to a bleak story. Although the author and publishers were prosecuted for anti-religious, anti-moral attitudes, would you agree that the story has a moral? If so, what is it?

A STEP BEYOND

Tests and Answers
TESTS

Test 1

1. Charles' mother criticizes Emma for ____
   A. not loving her son
   B. her lack of attention to little Berthe
   C. spending too much money

2. When Emma first meets Léon, he's working ____
   as
   A. an assistant in a law office
   B. a county tax collector
   C. a secretary to a retired army officer

3. On the trip home from La Vaubyessard, ____
   Charles finds
   A. a new riding whip
   B. a wedding bouquet
   C. the Viscount's cigar case

4. The Bovarys move from Tostes to Yonville ____
   because
   A. Charles' mother lives in Yonville
   B. they think the change will improve
      Emma's health
   C. there are more patients in Yonville

5. Léon seduces Emma in ____
   A. the back of a carriage
   B. on the way to the wet-nurse's house
   C. in the Lion d'Or

6. Emma's bridal bouquet becomes a symbol   _____
   of
   A. her middle-class involvement
   B. everything that is wrong with her
      marriage
   C. the romance that Rodolphe offers her

7. Emma encourages Charles to perform the   _____
   clubfoot operation because she
   A. feels sorry for Hippolyte
   B. wants Charles to become a famous
      doctor
   C. wants to impress Rodolphe

8. As a cure for her depression, Father   _____
   Bournisien advises Emma to
   A. drink a cup of tea
   B. become a church volunteer
   C. do some honest work

9. At the agricultural show, Catherine Leroux   _____
   receives an award for
   A. the general excellence of her crops
   B. fifty-four years of devoted service
   C. being a wet-nurse

10. At the opera in Rouen, Emma   _____
    A. imagines that the lead singer is falling
       in love with her
    B. falls asleep
    C. daydreams about her life in the
       convent school

11. Discuss the theme of blindness.

12. Discuss Flaubert's use of symbolism.

13. What is Flaubert's attitude toward the middle-class?

14. Analyze Charles Bovary's character; give both negative and positive aspects.

Test 2

1. When Emma goes to Rouen every Thursday _____
   to see Léon, Charles thinks she's
   A. going to the opera
   B. taking piano lessons
   C. consulting Dr. Canivet

2. At the start of the novel, Charles meets _____
   Emma
   A. at an agricultural fair
   B. when she comes for a medical check-up
   C. at her father's farm

3. After she gives birth, Emma faints because _____
   she
   A. wanted a boy   B. loves Léon
   C. lost blood during the delivery

4. After Emma dies, Charles _____
   A. returns to Tostes
   B. lives with his mother
   C. dresses in a new way

5. Léon moves from Yonville to Paris because _____
   A. his mother tells him to
   B. Emma refuses to return his love
   C. he can find a better job there

6. A symbolic gift that Emma makes to Léon _____
   is a
   A. book of love poems   B. bedspread
   C. lock of her hair

7. Charles marries Héloïse Dulac because _____

   A. she shared his interest in medicine
   B. he felt he owed it to her
   C. of her money

8. Homais, the pharmacist, represents   _____
   A. a symbol of impending doom
   B. the struggle between Romanticism
      and Realism
   C. the new middle-class spirit

9. Emma commits suicide   _____
   A. because Léon no longer loves her
   B. after Rodolphe rejects her plea for
      help
   C. because she's afraid to confront
      Charles with her debts

10. At the end of the novel, Homais   _____
   A. receives the decoration of the Legion
      of Honor
   B. moves his business to Rouen
   C. writes the story of Emma's tragedy

11. Analyze the structure of *Madame Bovary*.

12. Discuss Flaubert's use of "double action" (counter-point).

13. Based on *Madame Bovary*, what is Flaubert's view of Romanticism?

14. Discuss Flaubert's use of irony.

ANSWERS

Test 1
1. C   2. A   3. C   4. B   5. A   6. B
7. B   8. A   9. B   10. A

11. You can write about Charles' failure to see into Emma's true character, and to recognize the possibility that Emma can be anything but totally satisfied with her life. He's blind, also, to the fact that she's having affairs with Léon and Rodolphe. Up until the last moment, he doesn't even realize or "see" that all his possessions are to be auctioned off in repayment of her debts. You'll also want to discuss Emma's blindness to her own nature and her inability to see through the insincerity of her lovers and the machinations of Lheureux. She's blinded by her own passion to the consequences of her actions. Discuss, as well, the symbolic meaning of the blind beggar, including Emma's reaction when she first sees him at the side of the road. You might also write about how Flaubert equates blindness with the narrowness and monotony of middle-class life.

12. Flaubert uses certain objects more than once to reflect the thoughts and feelings of his characters. Discuss his use of windows: the closed window as a symbol of frustration, restraint, and the monotony of married life and the open window as a symbol of the possibilities opened up by dreams, as well as of passion and freedom. You might mention that Binet's lathe is also a symbol of the unchanging quality of provincial life and that carriages symbolize escape. You might also discuss the symbolism of the two wedding bouquets, the Viscount's cigar case, and the blind beggar. The bouquets represent the fleeting quality of married life and the death of love and beauty that ends in actual death. The cigar case represents the aristocratic world to which Emma aspires in her fantasies. The beggar symbolizes blindness, deterioration, and the death that awaits Emma at the other side of the "window."

13. Flaubert felt that middle-class pursuits were geared toward acquiring material possessions, to the exclusion of an interest in emotional or spiritual life. Most of the middle-class characters in the novel are characterized as greedy, superficial, unfeeling, and only concerned with appearances. You can discuss the middle-class qualities of Homais, Léon, Lheureux, and Charles. (See the section on Characters.) Homais, for example, values knowledge superficially as if it were a possession—most of what he talks about is derived from second-hand clichés. Lheureux, on the other hand, is interested only in money. His dealings with Emma mark a confrontation between greed and passion. Léon's values, despite his romantic side, are essentially middle-class as evidenced by his timidity and conventionality. His involvement with Emma bothers him because it conflicts with these values, so he ultimately withdraws, plagued by the reminder that Emma is a married woman. Charles is honest but mediocre and dull, two other typical bourgeois qualities according to Flaubert. In Flaubert's eyes, members of the middle class were, at worst, self-centered, hypocrites and thieves and, at best, boring, plodding, and vulgar.

In your answer, you might also talk about the reaction of the people in Yonville to Emma's death, the triumphs of Homais and Lheureux, and the "good" middle-class traits of Charles and Dr. Larivière.

14. Charles is under his mother's influence throughout the entire novel. This close maternal tie indicates an inability to step out on his own and be independent. His marriage to Emma is the one thing that he does without his mother's approval, and this is perhaps the main reason why Emma is so important to him. His inability to understand her needs, however, creates an intolerable situation for Emma. He is everything Emma despises; he is boring and mediocre. He has no particular ambition, nor the talent, to become a famous doctor (though he is hardworking and honest). Discuss his reaction to Emma at their first meeting, and describe the first few months of their marriage. His naïvely trusting attitude toward his wife might be viewed by some as sheer stupidity. His willingness to let Emma control their financial dealings shows how blind he is to the very essence of her character. His lack of imagination closes off access to the thing he loves best, his wife. You will want to discuss Charles' transformation after Emma's death and the possibility that he was truer to the idea of love than Emma.

Test 2

1. B   **2.** C   **3.** A   **4.** C   **5.** B   **6.** A
7. C   **8.** C   **9.** B   **10.** A

11. *Madame Bovary* is structured around Emma's attempts at self-fulfillment through romantic attachments. Each of the book's three parts centers around a romantic hope and a disillusionment. You can start out by comparing how she felt before and after her marriage to Charles. Discuss her illness after the ball at La Vaubyessard and how that led to the move from Tostes to Yonville. Her relationships with Rodolphe in Part Two and Léon in Part Three follow the same pattern. The need for fulfillment is followed by the illusion that she's found her ideal lover. When her illusions are shattered, she withdraws into herself and becomes ill. After she recovers, the pattern begins again. You can also discuss other repetitive patterns of parallelism and echoing that add to the overall structure of the novel. This would include the comparison of important pairs of scenes like the ball and the country wedding or the clubfoot operation and the opera. You can write about Emma's recurring religious feelings, as well as other repeated situations.

12. Flaubert uses "double action," or co
a way of contrasting the values of Roman
those of middle-class life. You can begin by c
conversation between Léon and Emma at the inn o
night when the Bovarys first arrive in Yonville, and
contrasting it with the conversation between Charles and
Homais which takes place simultaneously. Discuss the
use of "double action" at the agricultural show when
Rodolphe attempts to seduce Emma against the backdrop of the award-giving and the speeches. The scene
at the opera is also an example of "double action": Emma's thoughts are described in relation to what's happening on the stage. You might develop an argument
for the possibility that Emma's affairs are also forms of
"double action" set against the stodginess and monotony of her life in Tostes and Yonville with Charles.

13. Flaubert was brought up in a provincial middle-class
environment (see the section on The Author's Life and
Times). Yet in his youth, he was exposed to Romanticism, and this conflict between romantic ideals and
bourgeois values dominates the novel. Nineteenth-century Romanticism was a protest against the ideal that
the power of reason was what gave meaning to a person's life. Romanticism emphasized emotions and the
imagination, as well as a search for the truth of one's
individual being. You can discuss how Flaubert's feelings and portrayal of Emma are a key to his attitudes
toward Romanticism. Ask yourself whether Emma, as
depicted by Flaubert, is a true romantic. Refer to the fact
that Emma gets her ideas of Romanticism from popular
novels and that her ideas of life are distorted into an
illness whose symptoms mirror the characteristics of fictional heroines. You might also bring up the question
of the extent to which Emma belongs to the middle-class
world she seems to despise. You can discuss the idea

w the evils of both the ro-
s and chose instead to em-
d work and dedication over
. Larivière, and Justin are
om Flaubert admired. Some
uicide, Flaubert was able to
rd Romanticism and realize
ife was his devotion to the
art of writing.

14. Irony is a device used to express something that has a meaning opposite to what is intended or expected. Discuss how Emma's fantasies about ideal love contrast with the reality of marriage and her affairs with Rodolphe and Léon. Write about Léon's seduction of Emma in the back seat of the carriage in Rouen and how this creates an ironic contrast to Emma's romantic fantasy of traveling or taking a honeymoon. Mention how Charles unwittingly throws Emma into the arms of her lovers, citing, as an example, his suggestion that Emma and Rodolphe go horseback riding together because it would be good for her health. In similar fashion, Charles encourages Emma to stay in Rouen to see the end of the opera and to travel to Rouen to take piano lessons. In both cases, he allows Emma the opportunity to spend time with Léon. Write about the irony of Justin's involvement with Emma's suicide. Discuss the irony of Charles' romantic behavior after Emma's death. Include mention of the ironic contrast between Rodolphe's attempts to seduce Emma and the speeches at the agricultural show. And don't forget the biggest irony of all: Emma's dreams of love and beauty end in disgrace and death.

Term Paper Ideas and other Topics for Writing

Emma

1. Some readers have described Emma as being "naturally depraved." Explain.

2. Compare and contrast Emma's love affairs with Rodolphe and Léon.

3. What is the importance of the ball at La Vaubyessard for Emma's life?

4. Trace the development of Emma's disillusionment with Charles.

5. What effect did Emma's experience in the convent school have on her later life?

6. Discuss Emma's attitude toward motherhood.

7. Discuss Emma's reaction to the opera in Rouen. What does her reaction tell you about her character?

8. What effect do Emma's reading habits have on her attitudes about love?

Other Characters

1. Discuss Charles' relationship with his mother. How does he feel toward his mother after his marriage to Emma? Does their relationship change after Emma dies?

2. In what way are Charles and Homais similar?

3. What is Charles' reaction when he discovers the letters to Emma from Rodolphe and Léon? What does this tell you about his character?

4. What is the importance of the blind beggar to the story?

5. Is Charles' lack of jealousy a virtue? Why is he so trusting of Emma?

6. Discuss the roles of the other important women characters in the book.

7. What is the importance of the clubfoot operation? How does it affect Charles and Emma's relationship?

8. Analyze the conversation between Rodolphe and Charles at the end of the novel. What does it tell you about these men?

Literary Topics

1. What is Flaubert's attitude toward adultery?

2. Discuss the use of the "window" as a symbol of both freedom and confinement.

3. Discuss Flaubert's attitude toward middle-class society.

4. What is Flaubert's attitude toward religion? Cite examples from Emma's life in the convent and her relationship with Father Bournisien.

Further Reading
CRITICAL WORKS

Auerbach, Eric. "Madame Bovary" from *Mimesis*. Princeton, New Jersey: Princeton University Press, 1953.

Bart, B. F., editor. *Madame Bovary and the Critics:* A Collection of Essays. New York: New York University Press, 1966.

Brombert, Victor. *The Novels of Flaubert*. Princeton, New Jersey: Princeton University Press, 1966.

Culler, Jonathan. *Flaubert: The uses of uncertainty*. Ithaca, New York: Cornell University Press, 1974.

Kenner, Hugh. *Flaubert, Joyce and Beckett: The Stoic Comedians*. Boston: Beacon Press, 1962.

Levin, Harry. "The Female Quixote," from *The Gates of Horn: A Study of Five French Realists*. Oxford, England: Oxford University Press, 1963.

Nadeau, Maurice. *The Greatness of Flaubert*. Lasalle, Illinois: Open Court Publishing Co., 1973.

Schor, Naomi and Majewski, Henry F., eds. *Flaubert and Post Modernism* Lincoln, Nebraska: University of Nebraska Press, 1984.

Spencer, Philip. *Flaubert: A Biography*. London: Faber & Faber, 1952.

Starkie, Enid. *Flaubert: The Making of the Master*. New York: Atheneum, 1967.

Steegmuller, Francis. *Flaubert and Madame Bovary: A Double Portrait*. New York: Noonday Press, 1968.

Thorlby, Anthony. *Gustave Flaubert and the Art of Realism*. New Haven: Yale University Press, 1957.

Turnell, Martin. *The Novel in France: Mme. De Lafayette, Laclos, Constant, Stendhal, Balzac, Flaubert, Proust*. Salem, New Hampshire: Ayer Co., 1951.

AUTHOR'S WORKS

Major Fiction

Salammbô, 1862

L'Education Sentimentale (Sentimental Education), 1870

La Tentation de Saint Antoine (The Temptation of Saint Anthony), 1874

Trois Contes (Three Tales), 1877

Bouvard and Pécuchet (posthumous), 1881

Letters

The Letters of Gustave Flaubert, two volumes. 1830–1857 and 1857–1880. Selected and translated by Francis Steegmuller. Cambridge, Massachusetts: Harvard University Press, 1980 and 1982.

Translations of *Madame Bovary*

Bair, Lowell, and Leo Bersani. *Madame Bovary*. New York: Bantam Books, 1981.

Marmur, Mildred. *Madame Bovary*. New York: New American Library, 1964.

Russell, Alan. *Madame Bovary*. London: Penguin Books, 1951.

Steegmuller, Francis. *Madame Bovary*. New York: Modern Library, 1982.

The Critics

Flaubert and Emma

We cannot help noticing that Flaubert displayed a marked reluctance to give due weight to what was valid and genuine in Emma. She was not, as Henry James alleged, a woman who was "naturally depraved." She possessed a number of solid virtues which were deliberately played down by the novelist. It was after all to her credit that she possessed too much sensibility to fit comfortably into the appalling provincial society of Yonville-d'Abbaye and it was her misfortune that she was not big enough to find a way out of the dilemma. We cannot withhold our approval from her attempts to improve her mind or from the pride that she took in her personal appearance and in the running of her house.

> —Martin Turnell, from *The Novel in France*, 1971

Flaubert's Style

In *Madame Bovary* the crux of the action lies in the contrast between Emma's sentimental illusions and the plain facts of reality. The contrast would seem to be clear enough; but it presented Flaubert with a complicated problem of style. For he did not believe that any spiritual perspective *really* exists to distinguish significantly between them; emotions and ideas versed, to find man trapped by his own discovery, knowing that his new insight into the real is based